The Thousand Dollar Hunt

J.T. Brannan

GREY ARROW PUBLISHING

First published as an eBook 2015

This paperback edition published in 2017 by Grey Arrow
Publishing

ISBN: 978-1540659620

For Justyna, Jakub and Mia;
and my parents, for their help and support

"There is no hunting like the hunting of man, and those who have hunted armed men long enough and liked it, never care for anything else thereafter"

- Ernest Hemingway

PROLOGUE

The barroom brawl didn't even happen in a bar.

Instead, it happened in Napoli Coffee, Albuquerque – a chic, upscale little coffee shop in New Mexico's largest city, famous for its fresh beans and free Wi-Fi.

I suppose I was breaking new ground – the first ever "coffee shop brawl". Maybe it would catch on.

In my defense, the incident was hardly my fault; after a few too many cocktails at Burt's Tiki Lounge the night before, I found myself inhaling coffee and burritos at Napoli in a desperate attempt to combat a hangover. Not even the smile of the beautiful dark-haired barista who'd served me had been enough to make me feel better.

I wasn't looking for trouble in any way, shape or

form.

But I guess trouble just had a way of finding me.

My dog Kane – a curious but effective blend of Alsatian and Mastiff, who accompanied me as I wandered the United States – was waiting patiently for me outside. There was no need to tie him up; he was free like me, able to come and go as he wished. I suppose the reason he never left me was because he knew I could provide him with a constant supply of food and water, and dogs are pretty sensible animals at the end of the day.

It was Kane's low growling that first got my attention and – halfway through my third burrito and fifth Americano of the morning – I sat up to take notice of what was going on outside.

I heard it moments later – voices, loud and aggressive, and then I could see them from my vantage point at the window.

There were six of them, early twenties; large builds that suggested some sort of college sports team. From the way they staggered across the busy road, narrowly avoiding the oncoming cars, sometimes slapping their large hands onto the hoods and roofs of slow-moving vehicles, I could see they were still drunk; probably hadn't stopped drinking from the night before, just partied all the way on until morning.

Horns blared at them, but they just laughed and shouted insults at the drivers and carried on walking; and it didn't take a genius to see where they were headed.

The front door of Napoli crashed open moments later as the first man entered, his cohort right behind him.

The violence of his entry, the door banging against the wall, caught everyone else in the café off-guard; wrapped up in coffee or conversation, nobody else had seen them coming.

"Oh, shit," I heard the girl who'd served me say to the guy working next to her, and I started to understand that this might not have been an entirely random choice of place for the young men to get their breakfast.

"Hey, Danielle!" the first man shouted over the heads of the people lined up in front of the bar. "Get your ass over here!"

As the six men pushed their way into the café, the other patrons were already either getting their heads down or making ready to leave; trouble was in the air, and everyone knew it.

I breathed out slowly, then finished off my coffee as I observed what was going on. Nobody was going to ask me, but I knew I might soon be getting involved anyway.

My pulse increased a little, but not much.

The beautiful dark-haired barista – Danielle, presumably – pointedly ignored the young man and continued to serve the customers in front of her, and I knew the snub wasn't going to be taken well.

"Hey Danielle!" the man shouted again, just as the first couple of customers left the coffee shop, sneaking out with their heads down. "I said get your ass over here! Now, bitch!"

"Look pal," the guy next to Danielle said, "we don't need that sort of thing in here. Please leave, okay? Just leave."

I admired the man's guts, but it was clear that he had misread the situation; what might have been a group of nice, respectable men on some days, had been entirely transformed by their drinking session. They'd probably been on the drugs too, speed or some derivative to keep them awake, keep them going. Their faculties of reason – and their perceptions of the future consequences of their actions – were shot all to hell.

And they definitely *weren't* going to leave.

By now, the first college jock was at the bar, customers pushed out of the way, and he reached over the counter and grabbed Danielle's colleague by the apron-front, jerked him forward and head-butted him square in the face.

His buddies giggled as the barista's nose exploded, blood flying across the counter, and Danielle screamed in horror at the sight.

That's when the action really started – hyped up by the first guy's lead, another jock saw a high school student grab his bag and get up to leave, and knocked him straight down with a wrestling-style clothesline that drew gasps from the other customers.

All of a sudden there was chaos – the first man scrambling over the counter to get at the girl while some of the braver customers tried to stop him, at the same time as his drink- and drug-addled buddies began to slap

4

and kick random customers around the room.

I blamed my own hangover for leaving it too late; I should have got involved earlier.

But I'm generally reluctant to get involved when I don't have to – the police are keen to get ahold of me as it is, and I try and avoid incidents which might bring me to their attention.

On the other hand, however, enough was enough, and it was time to put an end to this.

One of the jocks was right next to me, fist pulled back to hit me where I sat, just because I was there.

He never got the chance though, as my booted foot shot out from next to the table leg and shattered the young man's kneecap; as he hit the floor screaming, I knew his athletic career was over for the time being.

Maybe forever.

But I wasn't going to lose any sleep over it.

I looked over to the counter, saw the leader of the group kicking one customer, punching another as they tried to stop him getting to the girl; while she stood there rooted to the spot, terror in her eyes, and I understood the dilemma that kept her there. Her survival instinct told her to run, while she also knew she should try and help the others. Indecision merely ensured that she did nothing at all.

As I rose from my chair, I glanced outside and saw Kane, eager to enter and help; but I shook my head at him, warning him off. His intentions were good, but I didn't want to have to explain dog bites to the cops, if it came to that; they might impound him, and these guys just weren't worth it.

I calculated quickly, guessed that the leader – pumped up on drink, drugs and adrenaline – would have beaten off the customers and be up and over the counter within the next few seconds.

Between him and me were four more of his crew, their attention now drawn away from the other customers by the agonized screams of their friend with the broken leg.

They looked hard at me, and I returned it with a smile.

I had about a second for each one of them, if I was going stop the first man getting to the girl.

It was more than enough.

As the coffee shop clients ran for the exit, I sprinted forward and slammed a front kick into the groin of the first guy, boot sinking satisfyingly deep into the balls. Even as he performed a slow, eyes-raised-to-the-sky, comedy drop to the ground, I was already whipping the edge of my hand onto the bridge of the next jock's nose; it cracked open and the man dropped from the shock.

The third man moved in quickly with a tackle, trying to take me down so that he and his friend could kick bits off me on the floor; but I saw it coming and dodged out of the way, the big jock collapsing on the ground just beyond me.

Caught by surprise, the fourth man wasn't ready for the huge overhand right which hit him square on the jaw; not too sophisticated, but brutally effective, and the kid was out of it before he even hit the floor.

Without wasting a moment, combat memory telling me exactly where the guy who'd tried to tackle me had fallen, I picked up a wood and metal chair from next to the nearest table and turned to the point where I knew he'd be; and when my vision picked him up, the chair came crashing down right over his head, just as he'd almost staggered back to his feet.

He wouldn't be getting up again for quite some time.

My legs were already moving again, propelling me the last few yards across the tiled coffee shop floor to the counter beyond.

The group's leader was already over it, fully on the other side now as the brave customers who had tried to tackle him moaned, half-conscious, on the floor. He was right up in the petrified young woman's face, one hand gripping her by the throat as the other drew back to hit her.

I had no idea what his problem was, but I was going to offer him a quick, ready-made solution.

I placed my hands on the glass countertop at a run and used my momentum to carry me over, one leg shooting out toward the man. My heavy boot caught his back at an angle – I hadn't wanted to kick him straight into the girl – but it was enough to knock him to the side with a loud grunt.

As I landed, I quickly pushed myself into the space that had appeared between him and Danielle, protecting her with my body.

The jock recovered quickly and launched himself at me, going low for the tackle. In the small space it was impossible to side-step, and so I sprawled out on top of him, sinking my weight onto his back to bring him to the floor, hammering a knee into the top of his skull as he went.

I felt the guy's body sag as a result of the blow, but then his hands were reaching out again, grabbing hold of me, his face coming up to glare at me, full of hate and anger.

I saw his right hand reach back toward his pants pocket, knew he was going for a knife; and in that same instant I reacted to the new threat, jabbing my thumb into his eye to distract him; and as he squealed in pain, the knife half-out now and still coming toward me, I reached up to the counter and pulled down hard on the cash register.

The heavy metal register tipped slowly, and the jock turned to look up at the noise just as it toppled down, smashing against his upturned head and knocking him unconscious instantly.

I ignored the girl's screams as I reached forward, pushed the blood-stained register to one side and checked for the young man's pulse. It was still there, beating hard. He was alive, he'd just have one hell of a headache when he eventually woke up.

I stood, turned and looked at the girl. She was just staring at me, then back at the mess on the floor, then back at me.

"You okay?" I asked, aware that I could already

hear sirens in the background and that I couldn't afford to stick around.

"Yeah," she muttered, hand on her head. "Uh, yeah, yeah, I'm okay." She looked at me and smiled, and I was reminded again by how pretty she was. "Thanks to you." The smile widened, and I smiled back.

"No problem," I said, noting how close the sirens were now. "Glad I could be of help. But I've got to go."

"I don't know how to thank you," she said, looking at me closely, "but . . . I get off work at three. Maybe you could pick me up, and we could think of something?"

My smile widened. "I like that plan," I said, already moving toward the door as her pretty eyes followed me. "See you then."

And then I was gone; but I would be back at three, as promised.

After all, to the victor go the spoils, and I didn't want to seem ungrateful.

It turned out that the guy who'd tried to punch poor Danielle's face in was indeed a college athlete, a twenty-year-old called Tom Dwyer who played football for the University of New Mexico.

He'd spotted Danielle at a bar she'd been working at a couple of weeks ago, and had been on her case ever since; as a college jock, he just couldn't understand how she could resist his advances. It looked like he'd made inquiries, and finally tracked her down to her day job at Napoli. But he was too young, too immature, and –

well, let's be honest here – just too much of a dick for the dark-haired, twenty-six-year-old beauty.

Apparently I, on the other hand, fitted the bill perfectly, and I was rewarded by a spectacular little afternoon at her apartment, situated just a few blocks away from the coffee house.

She had another shift starting downtown at eight, but I didn't mind – I'd worked off the adrenaline of the fight in the nicest way possible, and I was planning on heading out of Albuquerque anyway.

We left each other at her apartment door, kissed goodbye, and went our separate ways. She'd asked me if I wanted a lift into town in her little Ford hatchback, but I declined; it would only draw out the farewells longer than I wanted, and besides which, it was a wonderful evening for a walk.

I watched the Ford chug off up the street, and – with Kane once more at my heel – picked up my rucksack and started walking.

Walking was what we did, Kane and I; hundreds of miles, perhaps thousands, wandering from one town to the next. No plan in mind, no final destination.

Just wandering.

Fixing things too, I guess.

Fixing people's problems.

Because in every city, town or hamlet we ended up in, there'd be someone who needed my help, someone who was willing to pay a thousand dollars for me to solve their problems for them.

More often than not, I learned of these people

through simple, written advertisements posted in garages, diners, grocery stores or bus stations; anywhere that people thought I might eventually pass by. It was a forlorn hope for the most part, of course; after all, what were the chances of me actually stumbling across their cries for help? And yet I was kept in work almost constantly, finding these adverts for my services in every new town I came to. So perhaps it wasn't such a forlorn hope? But I knew the number of adverts must outweigh the number that I actually saw by a colossal margin, and I often wondered about the people whose prayers went unanswered. Could I have saved somebody's child in Detroit, when I was chasing missing jewelry in Tallahassee?

But I tried not to dwell upon it. A part of me still believed in fate, both for me and for those that I did – or didn't – help.

What would be, would be.

Still, I owed it to the people who believed in me to search for their advertisements, and before I left Albuquerque for good, I knew I needed to go and check out the main transport hub for the city, the Alvarado Transportation Center.

It was funny really – I rarely, if ever, used public transport. Most buses and trains wouldn't let me travel with Kane, and so for long-haul journeys I generally hitchhiked. But for the most part, Kane and I simply walked. For instance, after leaving Albuquerque I would probably head northeast toward Santa Fe, a distance of just over sixty miles. Without stopping, I could make the distance on foot within twenty-four hours, but I'd probably stop off at a couple of small towns and spread it out over three days or more. I wasn't in any particular hurry.

People who wanted to make contact with the Thousand Dollar Man, however, seemed to think that I got around the country on buses and trains, and therefore often left their posters in transport hubs like the ATC. It made sense, I supposed – most people hated to walk anywhere, and probably just couldn't comprehend my lifestyle.

The transport center was an hour's easy stroll from Danielle's apartment, and I arrived before the sun had started its final descent below the horizon. It was still warm, and the area was a hive of activity, tremendously busy with people who'd finished work and were heading home. I liked to be alone, but sometimes a crowd is helpful; it makes you less obvious, if people are out there looking for you.

It wasn't that I was wanted by the New Mexico authorities, per se; it was just that – due to various things I'd been involved with over the years – I was a "person of interest" to law enforcement organizations of all types. A crowd would help me blend in and escape notice.

Kane wouldn't be allowed on the train or the bus maybe, but he came with me into the depot. There were no rules against that, at least; and if there were, I was happy to ignore them.

The building was only fifteen years old, but copied

older styles from the area like the Alvarado Hotel which had once been the last word in luxury before falling on hard times and being knocked down in the seventies. The adobe walls, large plaster surfaces and red clay roof tiles were in the Mission Revival style, itself influenced by Spanish colonial architecture, and it was certainly one of the prettiest transport hubs I'd come across lately; it was even topped off with a clock tower at its northwest corner.

Kane and I entered the madding crowd, pushing into the heaving throngs, citizens of every creed and color desperate to get home after a hard day's work. People in business suits competed alongside college professors to get their tickets, as day laborers from the sawmills pushed up next to them even as office secretaries and high school students joined the human zoo. The sweet smells of perfume and cologne mixed with stale sweat and body odor to produce an atmosphere that was thick and unpleasant.

As we walked slowly through the main hall, scanning the walls for noticeboards and posters, I spotted a little coffee shop and wandered over. I was a caffeine junkie, and needed my fix.

I waited in line, ordered, then waited again as the matronly old lady behind the counter prepared me a cup of house blend, black and strong. Kane sat patiently next to my leg, watching the other customers with feigned disinterest.

It was only after I'd scanned the customers myself and turned back to accept the steaming cup from the unsmiling old woman, that I noticed it; a green four-by-two card tacked to a small noticeboard to the left of the counter, all but hidden behind boxes of knives and forks, salt shakers and glass sugar pourers, sauce bottles and napkins.

The card itself was half-covered by an advert for a pet-sitting service, all animals catered for and best rates guaranteed; but the part I *could* see had instantly grabbed my attention.

The top right-hand side read "-LLAR MAN" in thick red felt-tip, and I casually moved toward the noticeboard, picking up the sugar pourer and "accidentally" pushing to one side the pet-sitting advert to reveal the card beneath.

My eyes took it all in within a couple of seconds, then I let the advert re-cover it and poured some sugar into my coffee; I didn't want it, but felt I had to continue with the charade.

"Well," I said softly to Kane as I sipped my sweet coffee and patted him on the head, "it looks like we're not going to be heading out of town just yet."

Because according to the words on that little green card, there was work to be done.

PART ONE

<u>Chapter One</u>

We met on the benches of a kids' playground, right on the edge of an old baseball field at Tingley Park. It wasn't too far away from the Albuquerque Homeless Mission where Kayden — the writer of the note — told me she lived.

The girl was apparently homeless, and had no telephone; the advert had said to contact her at the mission, and so that's what I'd done, taken a brisk walk over there with Kane.

The sun had still been up when I'd got there, and I asked at the counter for the girl and was given an envelope in return.

Inside, a handwritten note gave me the meeting place; I read it, and told the guy who'd given it to me to tell the girl to be there in an hour.

I'd done a quick recon of the site – a lovely little park right next to the Rio Grande Zoo, itself part of the larger ABQ BioPark – and had then returned to watch the mission, observing as a woman left alone just twenty minutes later.

It reassured me that she was alone – sometimes these adverts are just put there to lure me into a trap, either laid by the police or instead by someone I'd upset, looking to get their own back.

I watched from a distance with Kane as she entered the park, the sun now almost gone over the horizon, and continued to observe as she sat down on a swing to wait for me.

As she waited, I doubled back and checked her route for followers; finding none, I then checked the perimeter of the park, closely observing the other people strolling the grounds.

None of them set off my radar and so – eventually – I approached the girl as promised, Kane still by my side to offer an extra level of protection.

After the introductions – which included a quick pat-down to check if she was armed – we settled down to business.

She'd called herself Kayden, although I had no way of knowing if that was her real name or not. It was hard to place her age, too – she looked like she could be young, and yet her hair, her skin, her clothes, her manner, all spoke of her being much older. But life on the streets did that to you, and a combination of drink, drugs and general abuse could make a girl age an extra twenty years in six months.

She must have been aware of how she looked, for the first thing that she did was press the thousand dollars into my hands, perhaps worried that I'd think she wasn't good for the money.

The relief on her face as she handed it over was obvious, and I knew why – if she'd been carrying this on her for any length of time, living where she did, she must have become paranoid about it getting stolen. People in her shoes were often killed for a lot less than this, and the fact that she'd gone to the trouble of getting the money – and then keeping it safe, both from others and from herself – made me more than a little interested in her case.

"I can't tell you how good it feels to get rid of that," Kayden said with a sigh, looking around as if she still wasn't at ease, was still worried that at any moment somebody might try and get it. "And you don't even want to know how I got it in the first place."

I smiled at her as she petted Kane on the head. "I'll take your word for that," I said, and meant it – I really had no wish to know how she'd raised the cash.

She smiled back, and I could see her crooked and uneven teeth showing, blackened like the worst crack addict's. But I wasn't there to judge.

"Nice dog," she said. "What's his name?"

"Kane," I told her. "He follows me around."

"I like him," she said, continuing to stroke his head, Kane continuing to let her. "Reminds me of home. Before my step-dad, anyway." She looked back up at me. "But you don't want to hear about that," she said, "do you?"

I shrugged. "Not unless it has something to do with the job," I replied. The fact was, it might do — her current situation could well stem from run-ins with her step-father, and the thousand dollars might be for me to teach him a lesson in return. Maybe even kill him?

There were so many people staying in places like the Albuquerque Homeless Mission because of things that had happened at home, so many parents and step-parents that had abused their children, forcing them into leaving home too early, onto the streets where the abuse just continued.

But I didn't kill people for money, no matter how deserved it was.

I didn't have many rules, but that was one of them.

I waited for her answer.

Finally, she shook her head. "No," she said, "no it doesn't. I've not even seen the bastard for five years, and I'm past caring about that sack of shit." She rolled up a cigarette and lit it with unsteady hands, trying to steady her nerves. "No," she repeated, "it's about my boyfriend. He's missing."

"How long?" I asked, all too aware that one of my more recent jobs had involved searching for a girl who had gone missing more than three *years* before. I'd found her, but I never liked those kinds of odds.

She paused as she thought, puffing on her cheap roll-up. "A month or more now, I guess," Kayden answered.

I sighed, wondering what to tell her. It wasn't three years, but it was bad enough.

The fact was that people went missing all the time, especially homeless people. They were often itinerant by nature, drifting from place to place. Oftentimes they would upset the wrong set of people and have to flee one area for another; or else they'd be picked up for petty crime and be encouraged to move on. It might be that he'd been arrested, or even killed; it was rare to get positive IDs on homeless corpses. Her boyfriend might have been murdered, or he might have been knocked over by a car, and she would never find out about it.

Alternatively, he might just have had enough of Kayden and decided to move on.

But, I supposed, it was too early to second-guess, and I owed it to the girl to hear her out.

"How long have you been together?" I asked.

"Over a year. Thirteen months, maybe. Yeah," she said, nodding her head, "thirteen months."

"So you know him well."

"As well as anyone I've ever known."

"Was he in any sort of trouble? Owe anybody money?"

"No," she said adamantly, puffing hard on the cigarette. "No way, man. He wasn't like that."

"Did he live at the shelter with you?"

"He *did*," she said with what sounded like the beginnings of pride in her voice. "But a little while ago, he got himself a *job*." Her eyes sparkled, and I could see the pride now. And the love.

"What sort of a job?" I asked.

"With animals," she said, stopping to roll herself another cigarette. When this was lit and the first few puffs had been savored, she gestured over a fence toward the zoo. "His favorite place in the world," she continued. "He'd sneak in all the time. Couldn't afford tickets, you know. Snuck in mostly at night, but sometimes during the day too, he's real clever." I nodded, waited for her to continue. "Sometimes took me with him too." Her eyes misted over and I could see she was being drawn back into her memories. "He knew all about the animals, I mean *everything* – what they eat, where they live, even what they were called in *Latin*, you know?"

"He sounds well-educated."

She nodded her head vigorously in agreement. "Yeah, he's got smarts coming out of his ears. Even graduated high school, grades good enough for college."

"So what happened?"

"Drugs, I guess. Same old story, right? Got in with the wrong crowd, got hooked, lost what little money he had, stole some, got arrested. Life fucked, you know what I mean? I met him right back over there at the mission." She gestured with her head, back over the nearby rooftops. "I was into him straight away, you know? Smartest guy I'd met in a *long* time. Funny, too."

"He still into drugs?" I asked, knowing it was indelicate but also wanting to get to the point.

"No," she said with an unconvincing shake of her head. "No . . . Not really. Nothing hard anyway, not for a few months now. That's why I'm so worried about him, see? We had plans. We weren't going to stay at the mission forever, we were getting ourselves straightened out. Going to find a place of our own. That's why I came to you, why I put the advert there, the police aren't interested in people like T.J. and me, they just put it down to drugs or some other shit, you know what those guys think – 'they owed people money, had to make a run for it, or else got killed over something, body'll never be identified anyway'." She sighed. "It's good to talk to someone who'll actually hear me out."

I felt guilty for a moment, knowing that I'd had exactly the same thoughts as the police. But there was no point beating myself up over it, so I moved on quickly.

"That's your boyfriend's name?" I asked. "T.J.?"

"Uh huh. Well, that's what everyone calls him, his real name is Ben. His second name's Hooker though, you know, like the old TV show?"

"Right," I said with a smile. *T.J. Hooker* – I used to love that show as a kid. "So this job T.J. got, tell me about it."

She puffed on her roll-up nervously, then shrugged her thin, bony shoulders. "I don't really know," she admitted, before pointing over my shoulder to the walled enclosure of the ABQ BioPark. "But I think it was in there."

"The zoo?" I asked for confirmation.

"Uh huh," she said. "I think so, anyway. That's the thing, you see, he never told me what it was. But he'd been over to the zoo one day, stayed there forever, came back to the mission at night and said he might have a job, he was really excited about it. I asked him if it was at the zoo, but he wouldn't really say, said it was something to do with animals so I guessed it was at the zoo, but he said he'd have to go away somewhere for some sort of assessment. So he left, really excited, and I've never heard from him since."

"And that was when?"

"About a month ago now," she said as she took a long drag on her roll-up and blew the smoke out into the darkening sky. "Five weeks maybe."

I paused, considering the facts. Had he been offered a job at the zoo? It was possible, if he had qualifications and was knowledgeable about the subject. But then again, it was hard to arrange employment without an address. Would they have accepted the mission as his residence? And what about references?

I came back again to thinking that maybe T.J. had just wanted to get out of there, had come up with the line about the job to make things easier for himself, then just cut and run.

"How was T.J. going to contact you?" I asked.

"Via the mission," Kayden said. "But I've asked everyone who was manning the phones, and there's been no word."

"Have you asked about him at the zoo?"

She nodded. "I asked, but nobody wants to talk to me. And there was no sign of him there at all."

I sat back and looked at her. "Okay," I said. "So

what do *you* think happened to him?"

"I keep thinking and thinking about it, you know? I guess it's possible that he went somewhere for an interview, an assessment or whatever, maybe stayed there with a job, maybe they had accommodation or something. Maybe an outreach center for the zoo, some research place or something?" She shook her head. "But I *know* that T.J. would have been in touch, would have told me what was going on, where he is."

Tears started to well up in her eyes, and I shifted uncomfortably in my seat; I wasn't terribly good with emotional women, despite my years of dealing with some very upset people.

"So," she continued through the tears, "something bad must have happened to him, I *know* it." She wiped her eyes on a dirty sleeve, looked back at me. "I know it."

"Okay," I said, tapping the envelope with her hard-earned money inside. "Okay. You've paid the price, so I'm your man. I'll find out what's happened to T.J. I can't promise I'll bring him back to you, but I promise I'll put your mind to rest at least."

She smiled then, a weak smile but a smile nonetheless, and placed a hand on my arm. "That's all I ask," she said quietly. "That's all I ask."

CHAPTER TWO

The next day broke bright and sunny, and I found myself part of a small queue waiting to enter the Rio Grande Zoo.

It was right over the road from Tingley Park, and I could see the playground where I'd sat with Kayden the night before. I knew she was counting on me, and the thought was sobering.

I'd gone back to the mission with her after our meeting, where I'd used my charms – and a hundred dollars – to get T.J.'s file from the desk clerk.

The information was thin – residents didn't have to give any details, and any that they did give didn't necessarily have to be true – but it confirmed what Kayden had told me, at least. The paperwork – filled out in his own hand, which was neat and precise – had the name Benjamin Timothy Hooker across the top, date of birth September fourth 1992, place of birth San Diego. Parents not listed, which wasn't a surprise. I wondered if he really *was* from San Diego; maybe he just liked its famous zoo, and put it down for that reason alone? People at missions more often than not didn't want to be traced, and it would be unusual if· T.J. had been honest on the form.

The next sheet consisted of the scrawled notes of the mission's resident medical officer, who examined all new arrivals. Again, it tied in with what Kayden had told me – signs of hard drug use including needle marks, damaged nasal passages, slight glaucoma and seriously depleted bodyweight. But it also said that he had indeed been clean for a while, and also made a point of him being bright, communicative and intelligent – a potential success story.

But as I handed over my cash and strolled through into the Rio Grande Zoo, I realized that I still didn't know a hell of a lot about the young man I'd pledged to find – one of the very reasons that the police weren't really interested in cases like this.

The only really useful thing was a Polaroid headshot of the man that had been attached to the file. It had cost me another fifty, but it was now securely in my pocket.

My backpack was in storage back at the ATC, only a few blocks northeast from the park, and Kayden was looking after Kane. He would have been happy to wait for me outside but – with no collar or leash – I didn't want him getting picked up by an overzealous warden and impounded. I kept hold of a Benchmade everyday-carry knife and an extendable metal baton though; my empty hand skills were good, but you never knew when you might need an equalizer. I wasn't expecting trouble at a public zoo, but you know the old saying – it's better to be safe than sorry. And in my line of work, such controlled paranoia had saved my ass more than once.

As soon as I was inside, I looked at the map I'd been given with my ticket and made my way to the information center, which happened to be part of the administration block right next door to the entrance.

I wandered into the light and airy room and waited in line behind a young family with twin pushchairs as they asked a twenty-something male something about the restrooms. Minutes later they were gone – apparently satisfied – and I approached the desk with what I hoped was a friendly smile.

"Good morning," I said. "I was wondering who I should speak to about a job?"

"A job here?" the young man – whose name badge read *Soren* – asked, somewhat redundantly. I resisted the urge to say, *No, at the White House*, and merely nodded and smiled once more.

He looked me up and down rather doubtfully, and I knew why; unshaven and with worn utility pants and t-shirt, I hardly looked like an ideal employee. It made me wonder how different T.J. would have looked. Given his situation, I guessed he wouldn't have made any better impression, and it made we think again how unlikely it was that he'd found some sort of work here. But he was bright, I supposed, and maybe that still counted for something.

"That would be Mr. Ortiz," Soren said at last. "Is he expecting you?"

I shook my head. "I've not got an appointment, no," I said. "Might I be able to speak with him? I'll only be a few minutes."

Soren continued to look at me for a few moments, before picking up the phone and pressing a single digit, an internal number. A second or two went by, then I heard a muffled voice on the other end of the line.

"Mr. Ortiz?" Soren said. "Sorry to bother you sir, I've got somebody down here asking about a job, could you come over and speak to him?" A pause, then, "No." Another pause, some muffled talk on the other end of the line, then, "No sir, I'm sorry, I don't know that either." Soren listened some more, nodded his head as if Mr. Ortiz could see him, said his thank yous and goodbyes and put the phone down, looking back across the desk at me.

"Okay," he said, "Mr. Ortiz will be over to see you in just a few minutes."

I nodded my thanks, and sat down to wait.

With nothing else to go on, Mr. Ortiz was as good a place to start as any.

Less than five minutes later I was shaking the hand of a short, bespectacled man in his fifties, neat grey hair slicked back over a tanned forehead.

"Mr. Ortiz?" I asked with another one of my

friendly smiles.

"Yes," he said pleasantly, with only a cursory glance at the way I was dressed, "and you are?"

"My name's Hudson," I said, "Tom Hudson. Do you deal with employment at the zoo here?"

"Yes," he said, "are you after a job? It's just that we're currently full to capacity, unless you've got some sort of specialist skills we could use."

The look on his face told me that he thought this was unlikely, and I shook my head. "No," I said, "I'm not after a job."

He looked back over his shoulder at Soren, confused. "I'm sorry," he said as he turned back to me, "I thought you'd said that you were looking for a job?"

"No," I replied, "I just asked who I needed to speak to about a job. I'm not looking for one, I'm looking for the person who deals with them. And I guess that's you."

Mr. Ortiz began to look nervous at the way the conversation was going – no big surprise, as he'd come to meet me expecting one thing, and was now being thrown a curve ball.

"I'm sorry," he repeated, "I'm afraid I don't understand. What is it that – "

Before he could finish, I pulled T.J.'s photograph out of my pocket and held it up in front of him. "This young man came here several weeks ago looking for a job. He's not been seen since."

Ortiz looked at the picture, then at me, then the picture, then once again back at me. "I think perhaps we should continue this discussion in my office," he said finally.

The office was fairly utilitarian, a nondescript workspace that might have been anywhere. But at least it afforded us some privacy, which suited us both.

"You don't look like you're with the police," Ortiz said as he sipped from a glass of water, seated across a narrow wooden desk from me.

"Good guess," I said. "Let's say I'm an independent investigator."

"A P.I.?" he asked. "Do you have some ID?"

"Not a P.I., no," I said. "More like a friend of the family."

"So you have no real authority?" Ortiz asked, his confidence returning.

I thought about flicking out my metal baton to its full twenty-one-inch length and asking him if *that* was enough authority for him, but thought better of it. Sometimes the softer approach worked best. Not *soft*, mind you; just soft*er*.

"I don't want to take up much of your time," I said. "I think you know the guy in this photo, I think you've seen him before, and I think you can help me find him. If you can't, I'll just pass my suspicions onto the police, perhaps with a little story for the Albuquerque Journal along the way."

I held Ortiz's gaze until he looked away, shaking his head. "I don't suppose it matters much anyway," he said at last, looking back up at me. "I do recognize him, yes. He came in looking for a job a few weeks ago, just like you say. Don't know any more about him than that really, not his name or anything else. I remember he'd been picked up inside the park by security a few times though, sneaking in without paying. Hardly an ideal employee, I'm sure you'll agree."

I shrugged. "Maybe your ticket prices are too high," I suggested.

Ortiz smiled politely. "The ticket prices are just fine, thank you very much."

"So you turned him down," I said, getting back on track. "What else can you tell me?" He wasn't advertising it, but I could tell he was holding something back.

He sighed, toying with his water glass. "I guess you could say that the 'interview' got somewhat heated. He tried to tell me how much he knew about animals, how passionate he was, and I . . ."

"Yes?" I encouraged.

"Well, I guess I got a little bothered by his attitude and called him a deadbeat, you know, words were exchanged."

"And?"

"And there was someone else present during our brief conversation, someone who overheard it."

"Who?"

"I'm not sure of his name, I'll have to check. He wasn't here to see me, but had a meeting with the zoo director, he was just passing through when he heard us."

"What happened?"

"He stopped the kid, took him to one side, asked him a few questions. I heard a bit, the kid saying he was from the mission across the way, it kind of confirmed what I'd thought, you know? Surprised the hell out of me when the guy said he might have a job opening for him. Couldn't believe my ears."

"A job opening?" I asked, realizing this could be my first real lead. "Where?"

"I don't know for sure, but the guy works for Badrock."

"Badrock?" I asked. "What's that?"

"Badrock's not a *thing*," Ortiz advised me. "It's a *man*. Roman Badrock, an ex-army general who's opened up his own game reserve and safari park about an hour away from here, over near Laguna. He's called it Badrock Park, if you can believe the arrogance. The guy I mentioned, the one who spoke to the kid you're interested in, was here asking the director about sourcing some animals for the park."

I shook my head, clearing it. Had I heard him right?

"General Roman Badrock?" I asked for confirmation. "As in, *the* General Roman Badrock?"

Ortiz shrugged his shoulders. "I don't know much about the military, but yeah, it's *the* General Badrock, the one the media seemed to love a few years back."

Sonofabitch – now there was a name I thought I'd never hear again.

Roman Badrock was one of America's finest soldiers – I'd even briefly served under his command in

Iraq, back when I'd been in the Regimental Recon Detachment of the US Army Rangers and he'd been a Brigadier. I'd never met him – our pay grades were way too far apart – but had heard lots of good things about the man. He'd been in the thick of the action his entire life, from long before the first Gulf War, to Bosnia and Kosovo, then back to the Gulf. If I remembered correctly, he was a fellow Medal of Honor recipient for something he'd done during the invasion of Grenada, way back in the 1980s. Finally made it to Lieutenant General before retiring a few years ago.

He was a living legend.

But unlike many of his contemporaries, who continued to stay in the public eye after retirement – writing their memoirs, entering politics, giving speeches on the after-dinner circuit, becoming subject experts on the TV news shows – Badrock had disappeared from sight.

And now I knew why.

Badrock Park.

The thought of it intrigued me. "What sort of job did the kid get offered?" I asked.

"Not sure," Ortiz replied. "The guy just said that he might have some work for him, didn't say what, just that it would be with the animals. Didn't seem to bother him that the kid was homeless."

Interesting, I thought, filing the information for later.

"How are relations between the BioPark here and Badrock's operation?" I asked, picking up on unspoken signals from Ortiz. "Any competition?"

Ortiz scoffed. "Hardly," he said with a hint of contempt in his voice. "We're completely different. We are a serious research organization with a commercial arm. Badrock Park is commercial all the way. He's tried to recreate the African savannah right here in New Mexico, complete with wildebeest, zebra, antelope, even rhinos and elephants; not to mention the predators that go with them. The man's got cheetah, leopard, even prides of lions stalking the grasslands in that oversized ranch of his."

"Sounds like fun."

"To you," Ortiz said sadly, "and to lots of others besides. The place isn't even advertised, and it's drawing big crowds anyway, people who've always wanted to visit Africa but can't afford it, here they think they've got the next best thing."

"And don't they?" I asked, thinking it sounded rather like a case of sour grapes, Ortiz jealous of Badrock's success.

"I'm not so sure," Ortiz replied. "An operation on that scale demands expert management, and I'm not entirely convinced that Badrock has the credentials."

"He's hired expert help though, surely?"

"You'd think, wouldn't you? And yet your young friend was offered work, wasn't he? And no matter his passion for animals, he would hardly qualify as an 'expert' at any proper establishment. There are lots of rumors about the general employing many of his workers from across the border too."

"Illegals?" I asked, and Ortiz gave another of his

34

casual shrugs.

"It seems that way," he said noncommittally, "although nothing official ever gets said about it. He has plenty of security there too, employs a lot of ex-military personnel."

"You think it's not well-managed?"

"Let's just say that our director turned down the requests of Badrock's representative the other week – we will never supply animals to that park, at least under its current ownership."

"Can you give me some more details?" I asked, my interest aroused.

"Details?" he said as he toyed with his glass of water. "Hell, okay, why not?" He looked back up at me, his eyes meeting mine. "That crazy general has gone and put the predators and prey animals in the same compounds, 'let nature take its course', he says – you know, lions and crocodiles alongside buffalo and gazelle."

I shrugged. "You don't approve of that?"

"*Nobody* approves of it!" he said in amazement. "I'll tell you what he wants, he wants the park to be part of some sick blood sport, get people to pay to watch the animals kill one another."

"But isn't that what happens in nature?" I asked innocently. "Why shouldn't a park, or a nature reserve, replicate that?"

"Let me give you two good reasons," Ortiz said immediately, holding up his index finger. "One, the animals going there are supposed to be looked after, as part of the park's commitment to the environment, it's supposed to be protecting these animals. Are you going to donate a zebra to Badrock Park if you know that it might get dragged underwater and ripped to pieces by a Nile crocodile a day later?" He shook his head. "I don't think so." He held up a second finger. "Two, Badrock is making a spectacle of nature, bringing out the worst in people and therefore bringing everything we do, everything we've struggled for and campaigned for over the years, into disrepute. It's like the damned Roman circus up there."

"But it's legal?"

"He's greased the right palms alright," Ortiz said dismissively, "he's got all the right licenses, yeah. Amazing what you can do if you have enough money. But we're appealing to the state government about it, and we'll go higher if we have to, believe me."

"Okay," I said, standing up and bringing our little meeting to a close. "You've been very helpful. My interest has been well and truly piqued."

"You'll keep the police and the press out of this then?" Ortiz asked as we shook hands.

"I will," I assured him.

"Thank you," he said. "And I hope you manage to find that young man. If he's up at that damned circus, who knows what might have happened to him?"

"Thanks," I said. "I hope I find him too."

Then I turned on my heel and left the office, knowing exactly where I would have to head next.

Badrock Park.

CHAPTER THREE

The lion roared, only feet away from me, and I could count the huge teeth in its wide open mouth as the sound passed right through me, chilling me to the bone.

It was the closest I'd ever been to such a magnificent animal — according to the tour guide, a fully-grown adult male which weighed in the region of five hundred pounds — and I wasn't sure that the open-top jeep we were in was the most sensible platform for viewing him. On balance, I'd have preferred something with armored glass.

There were six of us in the jeep — the driver and guide up front, and myself and three other tourists in the back. I was sandwiched in between a young couple and an older, lone traveler like myself. We'd all paid a little extra for the smaller jeep, to get closer to the action than the larger tour buses allowed.

"Don't worry," the tour guide said in a thick South African accent as the driver edged the jeep slowly along, flattening the grasses as we traveled across the vast landscape at somewhere under five miles per hour. "Samson here's pretty lazy, he's not going to do anything, this is just his way of letting us know he's there, that's all."

Well, Samson was doing a pretty good job of it, I had to admit.

And, as the lion padded gently alongside us, his muscles rippling and his mane swinging, I also had to admit that I was rather enjoying myself here at Badrock Park.

I'd arrived that morning, having hitched a lift along Interstate 40 with a long-distance trucker on his way to LA. I'd got out at Laguna, then waited for the transport which bused people the fifteen miles further north to the safari park itself.

I'd picked Kane up from Kayden, and he'd come with me as far as the front gate but – like the Rio Grande Zoo – they wouldn't allow him in the park itself due to "animal welfare". I didn't know whose welfare we were being concerned about – Kane's or the park animals' – but I agreed to leave him at the kennels provided. He didn't seem bothered; he probably welcomed a proper bed after a lifetime of walking and sleeping out under the stars.

I'd decided to do the tourist bit first, get an idea of the layout of the park, see what I could ascertain about the security here.

I could see straight away that Ortiz had been right about Badrock hiring ex-military personnel; there were a hell of a lot of former soldiers here, you could tell straight away from the way they held themselves, the way they moved. But perhaps in a place where predators and prey mingled freely – and with fee-paying humans also in the mix – having a good security team was a pretty sensible precaution.

Ortiz had also been right about the rest of the hired help, at least around the main entrance, animal houses and recreation facilities near the front gate. I didn't know whether they were illegals or not, but there were plenty of Mexicans here.

But on the whole – despite Ortiz's misgivings – the park was impressive and the general seemed to have invested a huge amount of money in the place. It bore out what I'd read in an internet café back in Albuquerque the night before, when I'd done a little research on Badrock and his safari park.

Badrock had retired five years ago, after thirty-three years of service to his country. Born in 1960, he'd joined as a boy soldier aged seventeen; a move that had surprised both his parents and their wealthy and influential friends. His father was a rich oil baron, and it was assumed that Roman would grow up to take over the family business. Even after he signed up, people thought he would just serve out a short-term contract and then go back to the oilfields.

But then came active service in the Sinai, El Salvador and Lebanon, until – just before his short-term commission was due to finish – he led a platoon of paratroopers into Grenada as a Captain in the 82nd Airborne Division. And it was there – after extricating three of his wounded soldiers from a gun battle with two bullets in one of his own legs, killing or wounding thirteen enemy combatants as he went – that Roman Badrock's legend started to be formed, cemented by the awarding of the Medal of Honor at a congressional ceremony a few months later.

It also gave Badrock a taste for action that he knew would never be satisfied in the civilian world; and so a short-term commission became long term, and the powers-that-be had marked the man out for great things, a fast-track career to high office.

At some stage during that fast-track, lengthy and impressive career, both of Badrock's parents died and – with no siblings to split the inheritance with – he became a wealthy man. And over the years, according to the *Wall Street Journal* piece I'd read online, he'd used that money to become even *more* wealthy, investing profits from the oil company into a burgeoning property and business portfolio that – back in 1999 – had put his net worth at over four hundred million dollars.

There was scant information about his family life, but it appeared that he'd been married late, although it hadn't lasted; his wife had been killed in a car crash while well over the legal limit, a tragic end to their short relationship. Their marriage had left him with a daughter however, so at least some good had come of it.

Badrock's retirement – even after thirty-three years

– had come as something of a surprise to many, as he'd been on the road to making full General, with a place on the Joint Chiefs of Staff. The military was in his blood, a part of him that ran deeper than any other, and in several articles, he'd claimed that he had the desire to serve until he was no longer allowed to. But despite searching everything I could, there was no solid information anywhere as to what had eventually changed the man's mind.

It was an interesting anomaly and I contacted an old friend of mine in Army records to see if she could provide me with any more detailed "insider" information on the good general. She agreed to try but – given the man's importance and super-high security clearances – it would take some time to get it to me. With no way of her contacting me direct, I said I'd check in with her in a couple of days to see what she'd managed to find out.

Whatever the reason though, Roman Badrock *had* retired and – in between conducting various business deals and arranging high-value security contracts – he had purchased a huge cattle ranch in New Mexico, fifty thousand acres of land that incorporated sandstone bluffs, huge mesas, rock formations, open valleys and huge swathes of expansive grassland.

It was here – at the re-named "Badrock Park" – that he immediately set about moving the cattle operations to surrounding ranches and converting the seventy square miles of land into a gigantic nature reserve.

An article in *Time* gave some indication as to the reasons behind his move –

"I've been around, you know? I've seen the best the world has to offer, and I've seen the worst. But what stood out for me, many times during my career, was the effect we humans were having on the landscape, on the natural world. Have you ever seen what Agent Orange does to a jungle? What artillery and mortar fire does to forest or grassland? Conflict all over the world comes at a cost, and not all of it is human cost; the damage to nature is extraordinary. And whereas we can make those decisions ourselves, wild animals cannot. And that's why I'm creating Badrock Park, to provide a refuge for some of these animals who are struggling to survive in warzones and conflict areas around the world, give them a safe haven, if you will. For it would be a true tragedy if we were to lose some of these species as a result of our own barbarism and bloodlust."

I guess I'd been impressed by those words, if a little surprised – it wasn't every day that a man whose money came from oil spoke out in favor of the environment.

But, as I joined the small group on the jeep as it headed out into the park, the sun already warm over our heads, the proof of Badrock's intentions was plain to see. The park was, as advertised, an almost perfect replica of the African savannah, the grasslands interspersed with occasional trees, giving way to higher ground beyond; and just like on the African plains, herds of elephants coexisted alongside wildebeest, buffalo, giraffe, zebra, gazelle and hippopotamus. They were all here, ready and waiting to be seen by the hordes of eager tourists; and yet even though the parking lot was full and I'd passed by hundreds of families at the entrance, out here we could barely see another human because the ranch was so vast.

Somewhere in front of us was a large tour bus filled with eager onlookers – I knew this because I'd seen it leave about ten minutes before our jeep – but it was nowhere to be seen now, and I easily imagine myself almost alone on the Serengeti. And at a fraction of the cost of a trip to Africa, I could see why Badrock Park was so popular.

It was true what Ortiz had said back in Albuquerque – Badrock's idea of mixing predators and prey was controversial to say the least. Apparently, some people – including the directors of most zoos in the United States – were up in arms over the affair. On the other hand though, there were many that approved of Badrock's maverick stance, claiming that a natural approach was the best to follow and citing the success of Africa's own game reserves as proof of how it could work. Badrock Park was a much smaller operation perhaps, but a lot of people believed that the principle should hold true there as much as it did at Kruger or Okavango.

There wasn't much of the circus about it either, if truth be told. From Ortiz's description, I had envisaged crowds baying for blood as buffalo were herded toward the water's edge, to be attacked en masse by crocodiles. But instead it was just as Badrock himself claimed – nature taking its course. He had just invited people onto the property to watch it happen, but he wasn't manufacturing any of it.

Safety concerns from local residents about the predators escaping were groundless – as well as fifteen-foot high double boundary fencing running the entire forty-mile perimeter of the ranch, the rivers flowing through the property were also netted to prevent the crocodiles leaving, while allowing fish and smaller marine animals to move through.

The male lion was far behind us now, and I felt the bumpy ride of the jeep easing up as we came to a stop.
"There," the guide said in his strong accent, pointing across the grasslands to a stand of trees in the distance.
The other three passengers and I moved to the side of the jeep and raised our binoculars to get a closer look at the troop of giraffes eating leaves from the tree branches, incredibly long necks at full stretch to reach the tastiest and most nutritious specimens.

"Wow," the girl next to me said to her boyfriend, "they're amazing."

"I know, honey," the guy replied, mesmerized by the scene. "I know."

"Those four that you can see are fully grown adults," the guide said, "about twenty-one foot – hold on." The guide interrupted himself as his own field glasses swept left. "Look," he said, "we've got zebra as well, a whole herd of them coming up."

We all dutifully looked left, and were rewarded with the wonderful sight of about two dozen zebra moving gracefully across the grass.

"And if you look closely," the guide continued,

"about a kilometer further off and slightly to the right, you'll see a small parade of elephant too, I see six of them."

I adjusted the focus on my binoculars and had a look. "Seven," I said after a quick count.

There was a brief pause, then the guide nodded. "Yeah, seven mate, you're right. Good eyes."

"Thanks," I said. I knew my years of close target observation in the Rangers would come in handy one day.

It was then that my peripheral vision caught movement, and I swung the binoculars toward it. "What was that?" I said as I saw the grass move again.

"Where?" the girl next to me asked. "Where?"

But the guide had already seen it, and nodded his head in seeming satisfaction. "Where the prey goes, the predators follow," he chuckled to himself.

"Leopard?" the single guy asked, but the tour guide shook his head.

"Dogs," I said, picking them up now, my eyesight just as keen as it had been on operations more than a decade before.

"Yeah," the guide agreed. "African wild dogs. They hunt in packs, bloody efficient too."

The guide had barely finished speaking when six dogs broke from the cover of the high grass and raced for the zebra herd, scattering it in wild panic. They immediately locked onto the slowest animal, left confused and seemingly dazed by the escape of the herd; when it ran, the six dogs were right behind it.

Despite its confusion, the zebra was still fast and looked as if it might outrun the dogs, but still they kept on in dogged pursuit. The zebra tried to swerve to the right, but two more dogs were there waiting for it, and it veered immediately to the left instead; but as it raced that way, another two dogs emerged, forcing the animals back onto the straight, right toward a small stand of trees.

"They're funneling it," I said, and the tour guide nodded.

"Yeah," he confirmed, "that's how they do it. Clever little buggers."

The zebra, despite the endurance of the dogs chasing it, was opening up its lead as it reached the trees; but then as soon as it got there, four dogs – which had been hiding in wait – leaped out from cover and pounced onto the racing zebra, jaws pinching around its back legs and belly, hanging on as the animal reared and bucked and kicked out wildly. But it was no good, as the rest of the pack arrived and jumped onto the zebra, bringing it down to the ground where two of them latched onto its throat.

A minute or two later, the zebra stopped moving and the feast began, the dogs working fast to strip the meat from the bone, furred faces and jaws covered in bright red blood.

The girl next to me had put her binoculars down. "I think I'm going to throw up," she said.

"That's nature at its finest, honey," her boyfriend said, as he continued to watch in amazement.

"Fuckin' A!" the single guy on the other side of me said, obviously enjoying the gory spectacle. "That's what it's all about! Fuck yeah!"

I was left wondering what to think. A part of me admired the dogs' tactics, and their tenacity. And like anything else in the world, they had to eat. It was a natural process, and there was nothing wrong with it.

And yet the older guy's reaction had left a bitter taste in my mouth. Had Ortiz been right? Was the park's appeal due to this kind of blood sport spectacle?

Truth be told, I couldn't be sure.

But what I *was* sure about, was that I'd seen enough.

It was time to get some answers.

CHAPTER FOUR

"No," the man said as he handed me back the Polaroid of Benjamin Hooker. "I'm sorry. I've never seen him before."

I was sat in a comfortable leather armchair in the plush, modern office of Professor Donald P. Groban, the man Ortiz had identified as the person who had recruited T.J. back in Albuquerque.

We'd completed the tour of the park, and as the hours had gone by, I'd continued to be impressed. I still wasn't sure about the idea of people getting excited about watching animals kill each other, but I had to admit that the overall impression was of a pretty professional operation, which looked just as good as anything running in Africa. As far as I was concerned, General Badrock deserved every success with the place.

When I'd returned to the front gate and the visitor

center, I'd found the company offices and asked to speak to Groban. I'd had to wait, but had eventually been granted an audience.

Groban was the park's director of operations, the recipient of a PhD from Cornell and the previous assistant director at both San Diego Zoo and Singapore Zoo. He was obviously an expert in his field, and once again I had to question Ortiz's assertion that Badrock Park was being mismanaged.

There *were* some anomalies, though.

Such as the other person in the room with us, seated far behind me at the other side of the office.

He'd not been introduced, but I recognized his craggy, weather-beaten features from my online investigation the night before.

His name was Miles Hatfield, and he was head of park security. An ex-Delta Force operative, his pedigree was unquestionable. After retiring, Badrock had set up a security contracting company called the Vanguard Corporation, providing personnel to active trouble spots around the world to support military operations, as well as private security jobs back home. Hatfield – not long out of Delta – had been recruited into Vanguard during its early days, and was one of the organization's top men. At the park here, security was provided by Badrock's Vanguard group, under the presumably very effective leadership of Hatfield.

I was all for security of course, but even I felt that Hatfield's presence here was a more than a little bit of overkill. This was a man used to fighting the Taliban, Al

Qaeda and Isis, a man who had protected presidents and fought wars, a member of a Tier One special operations unit who was skilled in counter-terrorism, demolitions, sabotage, guerilla warfare and more. His last job before Badrock Park was assisting the Afghan police in Kabul, during which time his unit had faced suicide bombings, IEDs, mortar fire and angry mobs armed with machetes and Kalashnikovs.

So why had he taken this job at Badrock Park? Did he just fancy a paid vacation?

The simple answer was that General Badrock had probably ordered him to take it; and Badrock never did anything without a reason, which made me wonder if there wasn't more to this place than met the eye.

After accepting a cup of strong black coffee, I'd opened the conversation with some compliments about the park before hitting Groban with the picture of T.J.

He'd just denied ever seeing the kid, but the twitch at the corner of his eye betrayed him; Groban had seen him alright. I supposed I'd just have to tease it out of him.

"Are you sure?" I asked.

He regarded me with a cool stare. "Absolutely sure," he confirmed.

"That's interesting," I said. "Because Mr. Ortiz from the Rio Grande Zoo was sure that he saw you talking to him, about four weeks ago."

Groban's eyes twitched nervously over toward Hatfield, then back to me. "Then I am very much afraid that Mr. Ortiz is mistaken."

"So you weren't there four weeks ago?"

"I didn't say that," Groban said after a pause. "I just said that I didn't see that kid. I was there, yeah, I had a meeting with the director." He looked again over toward Hatfield, then back to me. "Look, what did you say your name was again? What's your interest in this?"

"My name is Tom Hudson," I said, "and I'm a friend of the family. They're concerned because nobody's heard anything from him since your meeting with him."

"Mr. Groban has just told you that he didn't meet with him," a deep and gravelly voice came from behind me. *Hatfield.* "So I think there's nothing more for you to learn here. It's time to leave."

I turned in my seat, looked at the man directly.

He was big, but not overly so; he wasn't a gym queen, but a man whose body was a tool to get the job done, entirely functional.

A dangerous man; I could see it in his eyes.

"Hello, handsome," I said, deciding to change my approach. Being nice hadn't got me anywhere; and the definition of insanity was doing the same thing over and over again and expecting a different result. I wondered momentarily who'd first said that. Benjamin Franklin? Albert Einstein?

Well, whoever it was, they'd been right; and it was time for me to follow their advice.

"I thought you were just there to look pretty. You know, Groban has the office well done out. Potted plant here, painting on the wall there. Random guy on a chair at the back, makes the place feel complete."

There was a moment's pause, as tension seemed to increase in the room almost visibly.

And then Hatfield smiled; but it wasn't a smile that offered any sort of comfort or warmth.

It was the smile of a predator, absolutely confident of his place at the top of the food chain.

"Wow," I said. "You're even prettier when you smile."

My own confidence was starting to trouble Hatfield, I could see.

It was a test really, to see what sort of operation they had going on here. Innocent, and they'd just ask me to leave – politely and without any trouble. Anything else, and . . . well, I'd just have to wait and see.

"I think it's time for you to leave," Hatfield said simply.

"I still don't have answers yet," I replied, still twisted in my seat so that I could see him.

"There *are* no answers," he said.

"Oh?" I asked with a raised eyebrow. "Then what are you doing here, Hatfield?" I saw the reaction at the mention of his name, despite himself – an involuntary twitch of the eyebrow. "What's Vanguard protecting?"

"Who are you?" he asked. "Who are you, really?"

"I've already told you."

Hatfield shook his head, even as I saw him depress a button on the radio by his side. "I'm afraid I don't believe you," he said. "But as head of park security, I'm going to have to find out."

The door to the office opened then, and four security guards entered the room, looking to Hatfield for orders.

"Please escort 'Mr. Hudson' here to our offices for a little interview," he told them, and I could see the looks of satisfaction on their faces. If they were Vanguard contractors, ex-military, I knew exactly why; it was the thrill of some action at last, what they were born for, what they craved.

They moved toward me past Hatfield, who was still sitting comfortably in his chair by the door, and I assessed them all quickly.

They all moved in a similar way, well trained and agile; their body types were also similar, hard and athletic and primed for action. They wore the dark uniforms of park security, and I could see that their utility belts held Tasers, pepper spray, extendable batons and – worst of all – Sig Sauer P226 .40 S&W handguns. Again, a bit of overkill for safari park security guards.

I could see that they were confident, though professionally cautious. The first two men approached me, one to each side, while the other two hung back, hands near their gun belts in case something happened. I knew that if I went with them, the "little interview" would take the form of a severe beating and possibly – like T.J. before me – my mysterious disappearance.

So I really only had one option left.

As the first two men got to my chair, I stood and turned, hands raised, trying to relax them.

But then, as they reached for me to take hold of an

arm each, I burst forward, ignoring them completely; and a second later I had reached the two at the rear, too surprised to have yet reached for a weapon.

But I already had mine out, the baton extending quickly as it swung toward its first target; it reached its full twenty-one inch length just as it connected with the head of the man to my right, the *thwack* of the cold metal audible throughout the entire office.

He dropped instantly to the floor, and the baton was already moving again. I'd followed through with the first strike, and now reversed the swing and came back the opposite way, smashing the second man up underneath the nose, the whiplash cracking his head back and knocking him out immediately as his broken nose geysered blood all over the polished wooden floor.

I'd checked Hatfield out when he'd entered the office, and he didn't appear to have any weapons on him, which made him – at this stage, anyway – the least dangerous of the Vanguard men. He was also the furthest away, and to target him would give the other men time to draw their guns and shoot me dead.

And so before the second man's body had even hit the ground, I'd whipped back toward the two ex-soldiers by the desk, burying my right boot into the gut of the guy to my right. As he bent double, I saw the second man going for his Sig, and I instinctively moved in, my left hand trapping his right on the holster, gripping tight so he couldn't make the draw. At the same time, my head bucked forward, smashing my heavy brow line into the weaker bones of his face.

I cracked the first man across the neck with the baton in a backhanded slice, dropping him heavily to the ground, then whipped a knee up into the other guy's balls.

He gasped and sagged, and I span him around and rammed his head down onto the edge of the desk, finishing him off.

The altercation had only lasted a few seconds, and Groban was struggling to deal with the shock, eyes wide in panic.

I knew that Hatfield would be quicker to recover though, and didn't stop moving; and instead of turning to face him, I threw myself into a roll across the desk top, pulling out my Benchmade knife as I went.

My feet hit the ground on the other side and – dropping the baton – I turned, my arm wrapping itself around Groban's neck and pulling him from his chair, the knife's three-inch blade pressed hard to the man's jugular.

I finally looked across the room and saw that Hatfield was on his feet, the unnerving, icy smile back on his face, a small H&K USP Compact in his hands. The man was good – I'd not spotted the gun on him earlier, which meant he was practiced in concealment. Fast, too.

But now we had ourselves a stalemate.

I was careful to angle Groban's body in front of me to minimize Hatfield's options; if he took a shot, there was a good chance that Groban would get it before I did.

Hatfield still didn't speak, just kept aiming the USP at me as he stared with those icy blue eyes.

I had a feeling that he might just shoot, and damn the consequences.

And then the office door opened and I tensed, expecting a horde of Vanguard troops with automatic weapons to burst into the room.

But instead there was only the lone figure of a man, silhouetted in the doorway.

"Stand down, Miles," the man said in a voice that resonated power, and Hatfield reluctantly lowered the gun at his command.

The man came further into the room, and smiled; and unlike Hatfield's, this one seemed genuine.

"How about we have a talk?" General Roman Badrock said to me, as he looked at the carnage around him. "I'm always on the lookout for a good man."

CHAPTER FIVE

I sipped at a glass of port as I sat at one end of a long, heavy satinwood dining table, a plate of seared duck breast with all the trimmings in front of me.

All told, it was much better than being shot by a lunatic with a USP.

General Badrock and I were alone in the dining room, a sumptuous wood-paneled affair in the man's own ranch house, complete with chandeliers, expensive artworks, and luxurious rugs spread across its oak floorboards. Animal heads graced the walls around us too, everything from roe deer to grizzly bear.

"Your own work?" I asked, pointing to the mounted heads with my silver fork.

Badrock smiled through a mouthful of duck. "Guilty as charged," he said when he'd finished. "Hunting's one of the great pleasures of my life. I love the feeling, the cold steel in my hands as I lie in wait, the stillness of the moment, the clarity of the mind." He took a sip of port, savoring it. "It's like nothing else."

"That's surprising for a man with the career you had," I said.

Badrock laughed. "I'm an old man now, son. You know how long ago I last saw action in the field? It was as a major, back during the first Gulf War, over a quarter of a century ago now." He shook his head. "You get bumped up to colonel, to general, you know how many firefights you get into?" Another sip of the port, another shake of the head. "None whatsoever." He said this last almost regretfully; it might have seemed strange to someone else, but I knew what he meant.

"You missed it, then?" I asked, still not entirely sure why Badrock had brought me here but wanting to build up some sort of rapport with him so that he'd be less likely to call the police or – worse – have Hatfield come back and shoot me.

"I started hunting when I got to staff rank and it became apparent that I was no longer required in the field," he said in answer. "Believe it or not, I hadn't had any interest in it before then. It hadn't been part of my home life before I signed up, and then as a young officer there was so much going on that it simply never occurred to me to try."

Badrock looked across to the heads, evidently lost in the past. "It was a friend of mine, another colonel working out of the Pentagon, that took me on my first hunting trip, it was up to Alaska." He shook his head in wonder. "I loved it immediately, that first time got me hooked. You know what happened?"

He didn't wait for an answer, simply ploughed on with his tale. "We'd bagged a couple of moose the first day, huge animals. I loved the peace, the solitude, the feeling of man against beast in the wilderness. Then later that day, sitting around the campfire – and this was my first time out, remember – a giant Kodiak bear burst out of the trees just next to us, knocked my buddy ten feet to the side with one swipe of his massive paws. Then he turned to me," he said almost wistfully, "and for a moment – just for a moment – I thought I was going to die, and it was a feeling I'd not had in years, one which made me feel truly *alive*, you know? And then before I knew what was happening, a gun had appeared in my hands and I'd fired off six rounds. It was a forty-four Magnum revolver, carried just in case of this sort of thing, and those massive slugs hit the beast right in its center mass, stopped the bastard in its tracks."

Badrock picked up some more of the duck, placed it in his mouth and chewed on it thoughtfully. "My friend had six broken ribs and a punctured lung," he said at last, "but it was worth it. Introduced me to a whole new world, and I've been hooked ever since."

"And how does that tie in with the park here?" I asked innocently. "Environmentally aware nature reserve, where does the fix come from now?"

Badrock regarded me coolly across the table. "That was impressive, what you did back there in Groban's office," he said at last, ignoring my question. "I guess you must be something of a hunter yourself, no? You're hunting for answers."

"Do you have any?" I asked with a raised eyebrow.

"Yes," Badrock said, holding my gaze. "It might not be the answer you want, but it is the truth nevertheless." His meal finished, he poured himself some more port and stood, walking over to the massive picture window that overlooked a large swath of his property from the ranch house's elevated position on a steep bluff.

He looked out of the window at his kingdom for a time, before turning back to me. "Benjamin 'T.J.' Hooker is dead," he said.

I was taken aback by Badrock's words, his honesty disturbing. What did it mean? Was he telling me this because I was next?

"Groban met him at the ABQ BioPark, just as Ortiz said, offered him a job. You've probably seen for yourself, our staff here is a strange mix. We do employ some experts – and I mean *real* experts – for the more involved aspects of our work here. But let's face it, how much am I going to pay people to pick up elephant dung? And so I bring in certain groups of people that don't mind working for lower wages than the average – you know, men and women from across the border, or else people like Hooker, homeless and grateful for anything they can get."

He must have seen the look on my face, because he waved a hand dismissively in my direction. "Come on man," he said, "you know that's how it works. Some of the work here is menial at best, and there just aren't that many people willing to do it. So I've got to look elsewhere, right? And let's face it, I'm doing them a favor. Who else is employing people like Hooker?" He shook his head. "Nobody," he said in answer to his own question. "And they get well treated here, we either bus them in for free or else they can stay here in good quality accommodation blocks, they get well fed, and the pay isn't too bad, considering."

But – disturbing though they undoubtedly were – I wasn't interested in Badrock's employment practices; I only wanted to know one thing.

"How did he die?" I asked.

Badrock paused, sighed, looked out of his picture window and drank some more port before turning back to me. "He was trampled to death by a rhinoceros," he said.

"He was *what*?" I asked, genuinely surprised; it was hardly what I'd been expecting.

"Trampled to death by a rhino," Badrock said in confirmation. "Khuthala, one of our white rhinos from South Africa, five thousand pounds of him. Gored the poor boy too, tragically; the body was a real mess when we found it."

"What happened?" I asked.

"Hooker loved his animals," Badrock said, "he had a real interest in them – it was what Groban had noticed back in Albuquerque, why he'd offered him a job. But it made him reckless too, I'm afraid. The young man went out after the park had closed for the night, to explore for himself. But rhinos are territorial animals, and don't like surprises, especially at night. Hooker never really had a chance." Badrock was looking out of the window again, surveying his estate. "We didn't find the body 'til morning," he continued, "and by then it was a real mess, believe me. Thank Heavens it was found before the park opened though, could you imagine *that*? If a tourist had found him, we'd have been in the press for all the wrong reasons."

"Is that why you covered up the death?" I asked. "To avoid the bad publicity?"

"What was there to cover up?" the general asked, eyes back on me. "By his own account, he was homeless and had no family ties, nobody that would miss him, nobody that needed to be informed. He had no identification, and we only had his word for it that Benjamin Hooker was his real name. No social security, no driver's license, no address, no passport or birth certificate. He was a phantom, a ghost. And so we did what we could, had a proper burial for the kid. There's an old chapel came with the property, he's buried in the cemetery there."

I looked down at the ruby red liquid in my cut crystal glass and took some time to process what I'd been told.

The first feeling that came to me was one of failure; the boy was dead, and I would never be able to return him to his girlfriend. He'd been killed tragically, in an accident, then buried alone, a non-person with nobody to miss him.

THE THOUSAND DOLLAR HUNT

Except that somebody *did* miss him.

And how did I have any idea whether Badrock was telling me the truth? If I could prove that the young man was dead, had been killed as Badrock said, then at least I would be able to return to Kayden with some solid information, something that would give her closure.

There was one way to find out.

"I want to see the body."

Chapter Six

There *was* a chapel, just like Badrock had said. It was old and broken down, and stood a hundred yards away from a dilapidated single story home that had once been the primary ranch house, many moons ago.

The site was about a mile from Badrock's new, colossal mansion house on the bluff, hidden down some tracks in a small ravine, sheltered from the winds that would otherwise come in across the plains. In the days before double glazing and insulation, the location made perfect sense.

I'd traveled there in the back of a hundred-thousand-dollar Range Rover, Badrock in the back with me while Hatfield rode up front with the driver.

I was amazed by the man's confidence and composure – here he was, sitting within arm's reach of someone who had just demolished four of his men inside of ten seconds, and it was like he didn't have a care in the world. I could have been there to kill him for all he knew, and yet he had not even allowed Hatfield to search me; I still had the knife that I'd used to threaten Groban, and I could have sliced Badrock's neck wide open in a heartbeat.

But I got the impression that the general was so good at reading people that he knew — without a doubt — that killing him wasn't the reason I was there; and I also got the impression that he wanted to win my trust. And what better way than by letting me keep my weapon, while offering himself as a target?

It was working, too — despite myself, I felt that I was being drawn to Badrock like a moth to a flame, impressed by the man's charisma, his easy confidence, and his sheer force of character.

"The house hasn't been used for years," Badrock said as we stepped out of the 4x4 and made our way into the grounds of the chapel. "The chapel's seen better days too, I'm afraid."

"But I can see it's getting some more use now," I observed, as in among the ancient graves there seemed to be several which were significantly newer. It suddenly became apparent that Benjamin Hooker might not have been the only worker to meet an untimely demise here.

I noticed, too, several open graves just waiting to be filled.

I then wondered — and I was amazed that it had taken me this long to do so — if that wasn't the very reason I'd been brought here.

To fill one of these new graves.

I instinctively jerked my head toward Hatfield, ready to move if he was reaching for a weapon.

"No need to worry, son," Badrock said as if he could read my mind. "You're in no danger here. I just want to clear this up, so that we can move on."

Even as he said this, the driver struck the earth with a spade he'd brought from the car, forcing it into the soil of a newly filled grave with his heel until it went in deep, before pulling it back out and hurling it to one side.

"Move on to what?" I asked Badrock as the driver continued to dig.

"Let's just wait out on that," he replied. "Put your mind at rest first."

I nodded, my eyes roaming the cemetery – for years used to bury the bodies of family members and ranch hands.

"You've had more than one accident, I see," I said as the hole the driver was digging got larger and larger. I gestured at the open graves. "And maybe expecting more?"

Badrock shrugged. "Like any enterprise, we've had some unfortunate situations," he admitted. "Some accidents during construction, others with the animals. We bury the homeless ones here, although on occasion we also bury folk from across the border, if their families can't afford to do it back home. Sometimes sickness takes them too."

"Doesn't sound like a good safety record," I said,

but Badrock didn't reply, merely shrugged as if to say *what can you do?*

"I'm done," the driver-digger shouted from the open grave, and Badrock and I moved over toward him. I peered down into the hole, saw the man down there covered in dirt, a coffin next to him in the pit.

"Open it," the general ordered, and the man did as he was told, unclasping the locks and heaving the lid up. I knelt by the side, saw the body as the waning sunlight hit it.

The boy was in grim repair, decomposition starting to occur despite the airtight coffin; and even from this distance, I could see the damage that had been done to him.

The chest was half caved in, the face ruptured and semi-crushed; but despite the damage, I could still recognize him from the Polaroid.

So, it was true – Benjamin Hooker was dead, and the state of the body seemed to corroborate Badrock's tale of what happened to him.

And yet the crushing damage could have been inflicted post-mortem to cover up the real cause of death. I wasn't a doctor, and I wouldn't be carrying out an autopsy though; it was sufficient that the boy was dead.

At the same time, however, I knew that it *wasn't* sufficient, that there was more to Badrock's enterprise here than met the eye.

Why were there so many other bodies here? How had *they* died, really?

It just didn't add up, and I knew my work here was far from done.

If I was going to go back to Kayden with answers, it would have to be with *all* the answers.

And maybe justice too, depending on what I found out.

"Okay," I said to Badrock, "I'm satisfied."

"Good," he said with a smile, nodding at the driver who merely grunted, resealed the coffin and began to fill the grave back in. "So now we can move onto business."

"What sort of business?"

"You're an ex-military man of course," Badrock said by way of explanation. "Special operations, from your performance back in the office. Obviously engaged in private work now, hired by someone to find out what happened to old T.J. there." He gestured to the grave as he spoke. "Well, you've found out, and now I guess you might be available for another job."

"A job here?"

"Why not?" Badrock said pleasantly. "The conditions are good, we pay well – *very* well, in fact – and I'm now four good men down, thanks to you. So, you could say you owe me."

"They were about to attack me."

"Were they? I watched the incident live on CCTV – it's recorded too, by the way – and all they were doing was walking across the room. You attacked *them*, drew a weapon against men who were at the time unarmed."

"They had *guns*," I reminded him.

"In holsters," Badrock countered. "And at that time, they had no intentions of using them. But I'm not here to argue with you, or threaten you. Like I said back in the office, I'm always on the lookout for a good man. And right now, I need you. You do private security work for money already, so why not come work for me instead?"

"What sort of work are we talking about?"

"If I tell you and you turn me down," Badrock said, "you must promise never to reveal what I've said to another living soul."

"Okay," I said uneasily.

"I mean it," Badrock said. "Think of this as a military order, top secret stuff from a spec ops mission you can't speak of to anyone."

"Okay," I said again.

Badrock looked around the ravine, back out toward the rest of his estate. The air was warm, and the only sound that could be heard was the earth being thrown back on top of the coffin.

"What is the main difference between a nature reserve and a game reserve?" he asked me.

It took me only moments to answer, and in that time I began to understand a little of what else might be going on here.

"Hunting," I said. "Game reserves allow hunting."

"Exactly," Badrock said with a wide smile. "Exactly. Now, you can go to Africa and get a hunting license and go and bag yourself some big game, right? And here in the United States, you can hunt elk, moose, deer, even mountain lion, yes? And so why not do the same thing in this park?"

"You allow people to hunt the animals?" I asked, although the answer was already obvious.

"I do, and they pay me big bucks for doing it, too. And they can hunt anything they want, if the price is right, from elephant to lion. We even mount the heads and provide secure transportation of the trophies to wherever the client wants."

My blood had turned cold, my stomach turning with disgust as the reason behind Badrock Park became all too apparent to me.

"This is the reason you started the park?" I asked. "As a hunting ground?"

"Yes," Badrock said with a proud smile. "And why not? I can charge fifty thousand dollars for a hippo, eighty for an elephant, up to a hundred thousand for a lion. But it's not about the money, I have enough anyway; it's about the thrill of the chase, the thrill of the hunt. Why shouldn't we do it? It's in our blood, in our nature; it would be insane to deny it."

I wanted to argue with the man, tell him that some of those animals were endangered, what he was doing was sick; I wanted to grab the man by his hair and ram his face down onto my knee, again and again and again.

Instead, I forced myself to smile. "Good idea," I said through what I hoped weren't obviously gritted teeth. "I can see why you need the security."

"Yes," Badrock said. "Security for the park itself — we need to be sure that nobody gets in after dark to see what it is we really do here – and security for the hunters too, to protect them from the other animals. Some important people come here for the hunt – politicians, military officers, law enforcement officials, even movie stars, you name it – and it wouldn't do for them to end up like your friend Hooker there." He grinned, and for the first time I could sense the insanity which gently touched his face in the diminishing light of dusk.

"The rate of pay for senior security personnel –and after watching you in action, you definitely come under that category – is a thousand dollars a day, and we provide food and accommodation too, which as you have seen already, is first rate. Vanguard offers all sorts of other benefits too, but my personnel officer will tell you all about that back at the ranch house – if you're interested." His eyes locked with mine as if in challenge. "*Are* you interested?"

I smiled at the general. A thousand dollars a day? The figure had to be a good omen for the Thousand Dollar Man. I also still needed to find out more about his operations here, and what better way to do it than from the inside?

"Okay," I told him. "I'm in."

PART TWO

CHAPTER ONE

I was seated once again at the dining table in Badrock's personal ranch house, being served roasted quail by an extremely attractive young lady in a black uniform which was tight in all the right places, and I couldn't help but wonder why I was being so honored.

What was it that Badrock wanted from me?

"You managed to see my men in those hills," the general said with a smile as he tasted his Chateau Lafitte. "That was impressive."

When I'd given Badrock my answer earlier that evening, agreeing to work for him, it hadn't only been due to the fact that I wanted to learn more about his business here – it was also because I'd picked up a reflection on the side of the ravine, maybe six hundred yards out. I would have been an easy target for a sniper with a scope at that range, and – now knowing what to look for – I spotted two more snipers at angles to the first, perfect for triangulating fire on the cemetery.

I hadn't realized that Badrock had seen me observing them.

"Thank you," I said after finishing a mouthful of quail. "I guess my eyes haven't succumbed to old age quite yet."

"You're too modest," Badrock said. "Only a man of exceptional skill could have spotted those snipers." He paused. "How many did you see, by the way?"

"Three," I said instantly, conditioned to answering senior officers when they asked questions.

"And where were they?"

Again, I answered instantly, reeling off a description of the men's positions as if I was back in the Rangers, giving a report on a recon mission.

"Very good," Badrock said, then his eyebrows furrowed. "Which unit did you say you served with?"

"I didn't."

"But you'll tell me now."

I knew it wasn't a question. "Rangers," I said. "Regimental Recon Detachment."

"Ah," the general said, "of course. You had to be special ops of one kind or another. When did you get out?"

"Ten years ago," I told him, before taking some more of the delicious wine. "Medical discharge after Iraq."

Badrock's raised eyebrow told me he wanted me to go on.

"It was a mess," I said, "an Iraqi translator gave us some false information, dragged us into a walled village near Mosul. Told us there was going to be a big meeting of al-Qaeda leadership, the army sent in an entire company from the seventy-fifth Rangers. It was a trap."

Badrock sipped more wine, eyes regarding me coolly. "New Year, two thousand four?" he asked, and I nodded in reply. "The seventy-fifth Ranger regiment was one of the unit's under my command then."

"I know," I said.

"Damn," Badrock said after a moment's thought. "That was a bad one. How many was it?"

"Twelve," I said. "Twelve good men."

"Enemy casualties were much higher, if I recall."

"We got fifty-six of the bastards," I said.

"Doesn't make it any easier to swallow," the general said, "but at least there was some payback." His eyes looked up, as if he was remembering something. "One of the recon boys bagged half those bodies himself, if memory serves me correctly," he said. "He was awarded the Medal of Honor."

I looked down at my plate, took some more wine, a gulp this time.

"You?" Badrock asked softly. "That was you?"

I raised my eyes to his. "That was a long time ago," I told him, and it was true; it was a lifetime ago.

But I still remembered it all too well, the blood of my friends over me, the feral thrill I felt as I fought my way up through the building full of terrorists; the pain as I was shot, stabbed, and went crashing out of a fourth floor window, a death grip around the last man, taking him with me and using his body to cushion my fall but only partially succeeding; the months of rehab on my broken body, my eventual discharge; more months of struggling to find work, nobody interested in my unique mix of abilities; my eventual release of everything tying me to a normal life, and my final transformation into the Thousand Dollar Man.

I remembered it all.

Badrock stood solemnly, raising his glass. "A toast in your honor, sir," he said. "I had no idea the kind of man I was entertaining."

I rose and we touched glasses, and we both drank deeply from them before sitting down again. "How lucky I am to have you here," Badrock said. "Who would have thought it? I said I had no idea of the kind of man I was entertaining, but that is not entirely true. I saw the way you moved in the office when you took out those boys there, saw how you observed everything that happened this evening, so aware, so switched on to what was happening around you."

I ate more of the quail, unused to receiving so much praise; especially from a general, retired or not.

"You are truly special," Badrock continued. "A man of your caliber, I can use you for so much around here. As word from my influential friends gets around, we're only going to get busier on our nighttime hunts, and I need real professionals helping to make sure it all goes smoothly. The last thing we need is a Hollywood starlet getting gored by an elephant, or a Texas governor being ripped apart by a lion. Or a presidential candidate accidentally getting shot by an overexcited chief of police."

"I should think that wouldn't be good for business," I agreed.

Badrock laughed. "It sure as hell wouldn't be," he said. "But you know how easily those things can happen, especially after dark."

"They use night vision?" I asked, interested in the specifics of how things were run.

"Of course," Badrock replied as the beautiful girl came back into the room, uncorking another bottle of wine and clearing our empty plates away. "We only use the very best equipment, military-grade stuff. We provide training too, but most of our hunters are hardly professional men like yourself. Accidents can and do happen, we just need to mitigate the chances as much as possible."

"And what sort of work do you see me doing here?" I asked.

"Working the hunts, of course. Keeping an eye out for any potential problems, keeping the animals away from our clients, making sure that friendly fire doesn't catch anyone. And now I know your background, I might get you training them too, before they go out. Teaching them how to use the equipment, basic tactics. How does that sound?"

"Good," I said. "A little different from my normal work."

"And what sort of work is that, exactly?" he asked

with interest.

"Private investigation," I said. It was near enough to the truth, anyway.

"I see," the general responded. "You work for a company?"

"I work for myself."

"Good. No need to hand in your notice then. Have you got any jobs outstanding, anything you need to go back to your offices for?"

"Only this one," I said. "I'll need to contact my client regarding the fate of Mr. Hooker."

"And what are you going to tell this client?"

I shrugged my shoulders. "The truth," I said. "He went to the BioPark looking for a job and was turned down. Witnesses have him heading across the Mexican border soon after that. Unlikely we'll ever see him again."

Another smile appeared across Badrock's face, this one the largest yet. "An excellent answer, Mr. . . . ."

"Ryder," I answered truthfully, knowing that my fingerprints were all over the place anyway, and that a man in Badrock's position could have them checked within hours. "Colt Ryder."

"Well, Colt," Badrock said, "never let it be said that I am ungrateful to my friends." He clapped his hands, and the dark-haired beauty that had been serving us reappeared from a doorway. "Sweetheart," the general addressed her, "see Colt here to his quarters, and make sure he has *everything* he needs."

"Yes general," the girl said as she looked at me

with a mischievous smile. "It will be my pleasure."

I smiled back, sure that at least some of the pleasure was going to be mine.

CHAPTER TWO

The tray hit the back of my head hard, and I only narrowly avoided my face hitting the table by getting my hands there first, with just fractions of a second to spare.

It was breakfast time at the Vanguard security accommodation block, and – despite the general's seal of approval – I was not turning out to be the most popular guy there.

I supposed it might have had something to do with the four contractors I'd smashed up the day before, back in Groban's office.

I was stunned, but that was never going to stop me; an instant after the tray hit me, I pulled one hand from its braced position on the table, grabbed the fork from in front of me, whipped around in my chair and buried it right into my attacker's balls.

The man cried out in a high-pitched, strangled scream as his eyes rolled up into his head and he fell to his knees in agony, fork still embedded in that most vital part of his anatomy.

There was only one guy, but I knew my response was going to create some more heat; I could already feel the men to my right and left tensing, getting ready to strike in retaliation.

I moved before they did, elbowing the guard to my left in a backward swing that hit him right in the face and knocked him back off his chair; in the next breath, I caught the wrist of the other man, stopping the table-knife just inches from my ribs, and smashed his face down onto the table in front of him.

I was on my feet in the next second, turning to face two new assailants running at me from the next table along. I dropped the first with a heavy thrusting front kick to the gut, then sidestepped the next and whipped a vicious Thai round-kick across the man's exposed thigh muscle, the pain from the scything impact putting him down immediately.

Another man went down from a straight right, the big knuckles of my fist connecting hard with his jaw; and then another hit the deck from a side kick to the knee cap.

But then there were too many people around me, arms and legs coming at me from all angles, fists and feet hitting; and then hands grabbed me and forced me to the floor and it was all I could do to cover my head with my own hands as the blows came raining down.

There must have been thirty guards at breakfast, and I thought they must all have been hitting me at that moment, and I could feel the weight of them crushing me.

Where was Kane when I needed him?

A gunshot rang out then, and the blows stopped hitting me, the weight stopped crushing me.

I heard shouting through the blood rushing in my ears, felt the men move away from me until I was just there on the floor, alone and bleeding.

"– the general told you he doesn't want him harmed," I heard a voice shouting, and as my vision cleared I could see Hatfield standing there, pistol in his hand. "Now back off," he continued, "and I mean right now."

The crowd slowly shrank away, murmuring and muttering to themselves but obviously not wanting to cross Hatfield. And why would they? Even if he wasn't their commanding officer and meal ticket, he was an ex-Delta commando with a loaded handgun; they would have been crazy to argue.

"Come on," he said to me as he approached. "Get on your feet."

He ignored the other men who were scattered unconscious on the dining hall floor, and stepped over the man I'd slammed in the groin with the fork, who was still screaming in pain, and helped me up with one huge, callused hand.

"You're not exactly endearing yourself to the men here," he said with a half-smile, "are you?"

I tried to smile back, though the bruising was already starting to make it painful. "They just haven't got to know me yet," I replied, and Hatfield chuckled to himself.

"Well," he said, "that guy right there on the floor with the fork in his balls is the brother of one of the guys you beat up with that metal baton of yours yesterday." He watched the man writhing on the ground for a few moments before turning back to me. "But maybe we'll leave the formal introductions for another day. Why don't you get yourself to your room and clean yourself up? We'll be starting work soon, and you don't look so good."

I nodded my head, and wiped the blood from my mouth. "Yes, sir," I said in agreement.

Although the company left a little to be desired, the accommodation was as good as Badrock promised. We were in a block close to the main house, a huge log cabin purpose built as a bunk-house for security personnel; but it was a far cry from the places I'd lived in during my time in the military. Here, we had single rooms with private bathrooms, a full bar with open fireplaces, a Swedish sauna and an outdoor hot tub. There was the dining room too of course, and I'd already been introduced to that all too well.

Turned out dogs were welcome too, at least if you worked here, and Kane had soon settled in to our luxury suite as if he'd been born to it.

The girl was gone, but we'd had a good time the

night before, and some more good times before breakfast too; Kane had been so embarrassed, he'd gone to hide in the bathroom.

I watched him look at me now as I limped back into my room, face bruised and bloody – but it was only a cursory glance, used as he was to seeing me that way. Just another day at the office, I suppose he thought, and he soon got back to the serious business of sleeping.

As I eased out of my clothes and got the shower running, I considered the fact that – even after the story I'd given him about what I would tell my "client" about Benjamin Hooker – Badrock surely still wouldn't trust me completely, might think that I'd only accepted the job in order to investigate further. Which was true, of course – I had no intention of going back to Kayden with anything less than the entire truth. But I knew I was going to have to do my best to appear as if I really wanted to be here.

There was also the danger from the other security personnel, as I'd just experienced back in the dining room. Some of them wanted me dead, plain and simple. They'd tried it once, and I had no reason to believe that they wouldn't try it again.

Except, I knew Badrock would order them to leave me alone, and who would want to go against the general? They'd had their shot and blown it; perhaps things would cool down now?

I wondered, idly, about the possibility of Badrock making some sort of link between me and my alter ego as the Thousand Dollar Man. It was unlikely though –

my name wasn't connected to the legend, even in that Washington *Post* exposé a few years back and – as far as I was aware – not even the FBI had put the two together. But even if the general somehow managed to make the link, then so what? I supposed he'd see me as a mercenary, which was exactly what he was after anyway.

I turned the shower off and left the bathroom, picking up the telephone on the bedside table. I dialed the number for my army friend who was looking into Badrock's background for me, to see if she'd managed to find out any more details about his mysterious retirement.

"There isn't much, I'm afraid," she said when I'd finally got through to her. "Just rumors, really. Apparently, there was some sort of family scandal, Badrock tried his best to cover it up but the chiefs learned about it and, well, it ruined his chances of further promotion."

"What sort of scandal?

"I can't find out, there's no official record of it. As I said, it's all rumor. But there was no disciplinary action, it wasn't that sort of thing at all, but there was some damage to his personal reputation that meant full general was going to be permanently out of reach. That's why he retired, because he'd gone as high as he was ever going to go."

"Thanks for the intel," I said. "I owe you one."

I put the phone down, wondering if the lines were tapped. But what if they were? Even if I was taking on the job for real, I would want to know what sort of man I was working for, and I was sure that Badrock would understand my near-paranoia; it was what kept men like us alive.

Ten minutes after the phone call, I was clean shaven and dressed in one of the plain black combat suits that served as uniforms for the Vanguard troops here.

I looked at myself in the mirror, readying myself for the day ahead.

It was time to go to work.

CHAPTER THREE

The morning was spent familiarizing myself further with the park property, and with the weapons and equipment the hunters would be using.

The other Vanguard men kept away from me as much as possible, and the ones I did interact with greeted me with a mixture of open dislike and – having seen what I could do – grudging respect.

I spent time poring over plans of the ranchland – taking in the relief, the boundaries, the geographical makeup of the place – before heading out in a jeep for a closer look, with Kane in the back and one of the tour guides driving. We followed much the same path as the tourist trail the day before, but with the advantage of being allowed into otherwise forbidden areas – animal holding areas and feeding pens secreted in dark ravines, vehicle hangers and resupply centers hidden in the woods, and hunting stations wherever there was decent cover.

Badrock had a great set-up for the rich hunters here, I had to admit; it was a professional operation, through and through. He was making it as safe as it could be for them, and I could understand why. At the prices he was charging, the type of people coming here for the hunts weren't those that Badrock could just bury in the cemetery of the on-site chapel with no questions asked. They were politicians and business leaders with big money behind them – and wherever there was money, there were people interested in those who had it. If anything happened to one of the hunters, investigations would be launched and Badrock would be out of business, perhaps even imprisoned.

I wondered why I was still there, why I hadn't just left and gone to the authorities, had the park investigated.

It was a no-brainer though – I knew I would be killed if I tried to leave. Badrock was charming and charismatic, but he was as ruthless as his reputation suggested. The snipers back at the cemetery were proof enough of that. Maybe I could sneak out with the tourists, but what then? The ranch was fifteen miles away from the nearest town, and that was small enough to be difficult to hide out in. No, I knew the Vanguard men would get to me. And what then? They were only hired hands like me, just doing their jobs; would I really want to be forced into killing them?

And what would happen if I *did* escape? I had no

evidence, it would be my word against Badrock's – and he was a famous general, whereas I was . . . well, I wasn't a general, anyway. Nobody would believe me over him. Especially if – as he'd indicated – some of the people who hunted here were the very people I might want to go to with the information. *A presidential candidate accidentally getting shot by an overexcited chief of police* was one of the examples Badrock had used, and I had no way of knowing if this was literal or merely figurative. Were these existing clients, or just an example of the sort of people who came here? Either way, I couldn't afford to take the chance of contacting the wrong person.

I considered the fact that the general might keep records – who was visiting, how much they paid, the trophies they bagged. It was more than likely that he did, but where would I find them? It was unrealistic to think that there would be paper records in an old metal filing cabinet somewhere; Vanguard would be sure to employ computer security specialists, and any evidence would be well protected on a hard drive somewhere. I was good at many things, but hacking into computers wasn't one of them. Hitting people with batons, yes; sophisticated network security, unfortunately not. I wasn't exactly a Philistine, but I wasn't far from it.

So I would do what I always did in these situations – I would play it by ear. And if I got the chance – decorated war hero or not – I would bring it all tumbling down around Roman Badrock's head.

***

I was back at the main station, not so far from Badrock's house, checking out the supply of hunting rifles, when Miles Hatfield strolled into the armory.

Kane responded immediately, hackles raised as he emitted a low warning growl.

"Hey," Hatfield said with palms held out in placation, "I come in peace."

I nodded at Kane and he retreated to my side, still keeping his gaze on the Delta Force commando but silent now, allowing me to take the lead.

"Well," I said, "I suppose we're colleagues now, right?"

"Exactly," Hatfield said with smile. He looked around the large room, with its specially-made gun racks and ammunition stores, then back at me. "So what do you think?" he asked with a raised eyebrow. "Has Bruce done a good job?"

The Bruce he referred to was Bruce Underwood, the armorer there. He was in the back, rechambering a Winchester hunting rifle for a bigger load. Previously a Small Arms Repairer/Technician with the Marine Corps, he'd been running his own specialist high-end gunsmithing workshop in Montana when Badrock had come to see him, apparently making him an offer he couldn't refuse.

"Well," I said as I looked down at the Ruger No.1-H Tropical Rifle chambered in .458 Lott, designed for taking down African big game, which rested in my hands, "he definitely knows his business." I looked around the armory, then back at Hatfield. "And I think that there are enough weapons here to invade a small country."

"You know how it is," Hatfield said with a grin. "The people we get here, they've got lots of different needs, we need a lot of different weapons to suit them. Let's say we've got a young lady, maybe five two and a hundred pounds, but she wants to put down a bull elephant. What's she gonna use? It's a problem, right? She needs a big load, a powerful rifle, but then, will she be able to control it? So we've got weapons here to suit everyone, and Bruce helps to personalize them to requirements. We don't want our clients to embarrass themselves out there, you know?"

"That would be a real shame," I said, as I put the Ruger back in its rack.

Hatfield laughed. "Sounds to me like you'd love it if they did."

"What can I say?" I responded. "I'm a mercenary, like you. I'm willing to take the general's coin, so I don't judge. Hunting animals isn't for me personally," I continued as I ruffled the soft hair on Kane's broad skull, "but I'm not going to stand in the way of people that want to do it."

Hatfield nodded his head thoughtfully. "I can respect that," he said. "Yes, I can surely respect that. We're paid to do what we're told, and not to ask any questions about it. Same as back in the military, except we get paid properly here."

"That's true enough," I said. "We've traded one master for another, this one's just more generous."

Hatfield walked to a shelf and picked up a Barrett .50 caliber, hefting its weight easily. But I could see his mind was elsewhere, the rifle a mere prop. I waited to hear what was on his mind.

"Roman says you won the Medal of Honor," he said at last. There was respect – even admiration – in his voice, but tainted by a hint of jealousy, a threat of competition.

"It was a long time ago," I answered.

"Well anyway," he continued, putting the rifle back, "it's a hell of a thing, it really is. We don't get that many Medal of Honor winners down here, that's for sure. There aren't that many of you *anywhere*, as a matter of fact."

"Not alive, anyway," I said, wondering where Hatfield was going with this.

The man chuckled. "I guess that's right," he said, before shaking his head in wonder. "Well anyway, Roman's got big plans for you, my friend. *Big* plans. You've impressed the hell out of him, you know? So you'll be staying with him in the house, away from the others. They've been warned off you, but you know how it is – boys will be boys and all that. We can't guarantee your safety if you stay in the block with them."

"Are they jealous?" I asked with half a smile.

"You could say that – word has already got out that you're on more money than they are, and a few of them are pissed about your roll in the sack with Talia last night too. Plenty of the boys had designs on that one, but nobody wanted to mess with the general's daughter."

My eyes must have registered my shock, despite myself. "The general's —" I couldn't help myself repeating, stopped by Hatfield's nodding head.

"Yes," he said with a wicked smile. "The girl you fucked this way and that last night was Talia Badrock, the general's daughter."

"But why would — "

"I told you, Roman likes you," Hatfield said. "And Talia is a resource to be used like any other. He *is* a most practical man."

My stomach turned at the thought of how Badrock had used his daughter, and I felt strong pangs of guilt myself. But who had I thought she was?

The thing was, I had just assumed she was a working girl, hired by the general. And I'd thought that that was okay, in its own way. But was it? Everyone was *someone's* daughter, after all.

But it was the sheer cold-blooded manipulation of the man that shocked me, his willingness to use his own flesh and blood to achieve his aims. But what aim did he have in mind when he sent me back to my room with Talia? What had he hoped to accomplish?

The whole situation bewildered me, but at the same time the beginnings of a plan started to form in my mind.

"Anyway," Hatfield continued, with the smile still playing across his lips, "the reason I'm here is to tell you that our next hunt is tomorrow night. And it's going to be an important one too, some real big name VIPs are coming here. They start arriving in the morning, you'll be on the meet-and-greet team, you'll help them with their weapon handling drills, make sure everyone's capable of being out there in the field without hurting themselves, or other people. Then when the park closes, you'll get to see the real fun begin."

I looked at Hatfield and smiled weakly. "I can't wait," I said.

The ex-commando's smile was much more convincing than mine. "I bet you can't," he said. "I just bet you can't."

CHAPTER FOUR

Talia Badrock was waiting for me in my new room when I arrived, already naked in my bed.

I dropped my things on the floor and looked at her. She was stunning, there was no doubt about it; olive skin and deep green eyes framed by curls of dark hair that fell to her smooth-skinned shoulders.

But I looked at her differently now, knowing what I knew.

"Why didn't you tell me?" I asked her.

"Tell you what?" she purred softly, eyes questioning.

"That you're the general's daughter."

"Would it have made a difference?" she asked, her expression unchanged.

It was a good question. "It might have," I said.

"Why?"

Damn – another good question. Her blasé attitude about what she'd been made to do by her father left me confused, not knowing how to carry on the conversation. It was unlikely I'd been the first person she'd been asked to "entertain". What effect would that have on a person?

But then again, she was an adult. Didn't she have a choice in the matter? And if she did, and she chose to do it anyway, then what did that say about her?

But then again, I knew firsthand how convincing her father could be. How much would a lifetime of brainwashing affect someone? Would she really have had any choice? After being under his influence for so long, was it possible for her to make her own mind up?

And even if he hadn't completely dominated her mentally, there were always the physical threats the man could make. How free was *I* to leave this place? If I tried anything, I'd have fifty ex-military killers on my tail; I didn't imagine that Talia would have it any easier.

"It might have made a difference," I answered her finally, "if I'd known you were being forced into it."

"But you must have assumed I was a hooker the first time, or at least something similar, you must have assumed I was being paid for my services."

"I guess so," I replied weakly.

"And that was okay with you." It was a statement more than a question.

"I didn't really think about it at the time," I answered, and it was the truth, too. The furthest my brain had got was *never look a gift horse in the mouth.*

Shallow? Perhaps; but then again, I'd never claimed to be anything else.

I spotted a fridge in the corner of the room and walked over to it, hoping the general had stocked it properly. I wasn't disappointed as I opened the door, and pulled out a bottle of Bud. "Want one?" I asked, holding a bottle up for her to see.

"Why not?" she said with a smile, and I bit off the cap, moved across to the bed and passed it to her.

I sat on the edge of the bed as I opened my own and took a large, satisfying gulp.

I turned back to her, her supple naked body propped up on the pillows, sheets resting in a silken pool at her lap. "I'm sorry," I told her.

"Sorry?" she asked with surprise as she sipped her beer. "Sorry for what?"

"I'm sorry that your father's been using you. Sorry you've had to do . . . the things you've done."

Talia regarded me coolly for a few moments, then burst out laughing. I was caught off-guard; the laugher seemed quite genuine.

"You think he *makes* me do this?" she asked, before putting the bottle back to her lips. "I'm twenty-two years old, you think he can keep me here?"

I looked in her eyes, trying hard to read her. "Yes," I said eventually, keeping my gaze on her. "Yes, I think he can."

She opened her mouth to say something else, then seemed to think better of it, drinking more of the beer instead. She tried to speak again, but the words wouldn't come.

I walked back to the fridge, pulled out two more Buds. "Fancy another?" I asked her.

She nodded her head, and I passed her one, noting that the sheets were now pulled up to her shoulders, her body covered.

I sat on the bed next to her, reclined back on the pillows and enjoyed my second bottle of beer, giving Talia some time to get her words out, not wanting to pressure her into talking.

"I can't leave," she said eventually, in a voice little more than a whisper. "I can't."

I still didn't respond, knew that if I just gave her the space, the words would come.

And, finally, they did.

"I didn't see my father that much growing up. Boarding school all the way, you know? Mom died when I was young, and he was a hot-shot army officer. How could he have time for his kids?" She shook her head. "He couldn't. And I didn't hold it against him . . . Or at least I didn't think I did. But then I made some choices, some bad choices, and I think I did it just to get his attention, get back at him somehow, you know?"

"I think so," I said gently, encouraging her to continue.

"So, I got into alcohol in high school, messing about with boys when I was too young, you know the sort of thing. My father ignored it, or maybe didn't even realize it was happening. Still made it into college though, but the drugs I'd started dabbling a bit with at boarding school got harder. First pills, then coke, but then I was smoking crack every day, running with the wrong people, and I mean the *really* wrong people, I ended up turning tricks to pay for it, working for a pimp who supplied me." She shook her head sadly. "My father finally found out," she said. "Or at least he finally *had* to pay attention when he was forced to bail me out of jail."

I drank some more of the ice-cold Bud to help soften the blow of what I was hearing, the liquid sliding wonderfully down my throat as she continued her sorry tale.

"It almost killed him, you know? Could you imagine the damage to his reputation if people found out about me? His drug-addict crack whore daughter?" She shook her head sadly. "The number of people he had to pay off to keep my name out of the papers, off the TV, it was incredible, as he kept on reminding me. He told me names, what he'd had to pay them, made me repeat it to him until he was happy that I appreciated what he'd done. He retired from the army too, I'd ruined his chances of ever making it further, and he never let me forget *that* either."

That explained the unknown family scandal that my friend had told me about, at least.

"He booked me into a private clinic too," Talia continued, "to clean me up. Eventually brought me up here to his ranch to start over, a 'new life', he told me."

There were tears in her eyes now, and I put an arm round her shoulders, her head nestling on my chest.

"The new life didn't last long," she said in a ragged whisper. "He said that I owed him, that I needed to work for him now. He told me that I'd proved what sort of work I was good for."

There was bitterness in her voice now, and who could blame her? The desire to kill her father, to wipe General Roman Badrock off the face of the earth, emerged like a jolt of lightning deep in my guts. But still I didn't speak, knowing there was more to come.

"I don't have to do as much as when I was on the streets," she said at last. "And it *is* a lot nicer here." She paused, deciding how to phrase what she wanted to say. "But at least on the streets I had the drugs," she said through her tears. "At least they helped numb the pain, I could pretend none of it was real. But here," she waved a hand around the room, "I *know* it's real. He makes me 'entertain' special guests, his high-rolling hunters, I'm like a free call-girl at a Vegas casino. And I know he'll kill me if I ever try and leave."

I breathed out slowly, my impression of the general damaged beyond belief, beyond restitution. A man who would prostitute his own daughter, who would *kill* her if she tried to escape.

Talia sighed then, wiped the tears away, and drank some more beer – at least a little something to numb the pain. "I don't know why I've told you all this," she said weakly. "You're one of them now, you work for Vanguard, you work for *him*."

The guilt flooded me, but the feeling was momentary; there were things that could be done to help redress the balance.

"You told me because you know I'm not like the others," I said as I held her tight. "Because you know I can help you."

"Help me how?" she asked softly.

"Help you get out of here," I said, stroking her hair. "But first," I continued, thinking about the plan that had occurred to me back in the armory, "you just might be able to help *me*."

CHAPTER FIVE

I lay in the long grass, feeling the warm breeze wash over me, the crescent moon above casting its silvery glow across the plain below.

I could see well enough just from the moonlight, but through the FLIR T75 long-range thermal sight mounted to my FN SCAR 7.62mm battle rifle, the images were crystal clear. But with a sight that cost just shy of seventeen thousand dollars, I supposed they should be.

The rifle wasn't exactly easy to get hold of either, purpose designed for the US special operations community. The first batch had actually been used by my old unit, the 75th Rangers, but it was after my time; I'd been used to the good old M4.

The new weapon was good though, and I'd zeroed

it in on one of the outdoor ranges earlier that evening. That session had actually turned into something of an impromptu shooting contest, and was the reason why I had the rifle, and the guy lying next to me was the spotter; it had soon become apparent that I was a better shot than any of the other Vanguard employees. The guys had bitched and moaned, but the results spoke for themselves and I was taking the lead on this little two-man fire team.

My spotter – an ex-Marine I'd buried in the shooting comp – was obviously still pissed, and kept his communications with me to a minimum, which was just fine by me. I'm not the most talkative guy at the best of times, and I had absolutely nothing to say to the Vanguard man next to me. He could scan the area in front of us, and give me a target to shoot at if any came up, and that would be it for our interaction.

Kane was out with us too, lying on the opposite side to my spotter, his fur warm against my skin. I would be more likely, I believed, to get a decent conversation out of *him*.

The variant of the FN SCAR I was using tonight was the SSR, the Sniper Support Rifle, and it was accurate out to a range of a thousand yards; but with its twenty round magazine it was also designed for rapid semi-automatic fire, and it was easier to get rounds down quickly than with a standard hunting or sniper rifle, which was why I was using it.

I was on overwatch duty, protecting the man who had paid Badrock one hundred thousand dollars to go hunting lion.

Ian Garner was an international banker, a big shot financial whiz-kid from the Big Apple who wanted to trade the urban jungle of Wall Street for the real one lying here in New Mexico, at least for a couple of nights. He was part of the hunting party booked for tomorrow night, but had turned up a day early. Not wanting to turn down his offer of a hundred grand for an extra night's hunting, Badrock had quickly adapted, and agreed to his demands.

Garner had explained to me over dinner that he simply didn't have time to get over to the game reserves in Africa, he was far too busy; and so why not visit the famed Badrock Park? If he enjoyed it, he would become a regular here.

The man made me sick to my stomach, and it had taken everything I had not to bury my fish knife through one of his bespectacled eyeballs.

But I knew that if I did, my chances of destroying the general's little hunting wonderland here would be seriously damaged. And so instead, I did as I was told – I went out with the hunting party, responsible for observing the area around the client from a nearby ridge, my own rifle primed and ready to defend him from anything that might be creeping up on him.

Would I shoot if I saw something? Or would I let the banker get ripped to pieces?

I still wasn't sure, to be honest. He was a vile little man who wouldn't be missed, but I had to be seen to be doing my job, at least for now.

There was also the fact that the general was right next to him, lying there in wait for their prey. If something attacked Garner, it would get Badrock too. And what a way for the man to go!

But I wasn't the only Vanguard employee keeping an eye on things out here – several more snipers were out and about securing the area, and I suspected that some of them might even have their weapons trained on me.

So I had to keep the two men secure, despite myself.

I traced my sight across the prone form of General Badrock, thinking how satisfying it would be to put a 7.62mm round through his spine. I wondered if I could do it and get away with it; shoot the general, disable the man next to me, and escape from the park before the rest of the men knew what was happening.

But I knew that such an escape would be unlikely – the Vanguard crew had night vision, thermal imaging, and they probably had access to helicopter support too, not to mention enough firepower to lay waste to half of New Mexico.

No, I decided in the end, there had to be a better way.

A way that would result in the good general getting what he deserved, and me getting away safe, sound and alive.

I considered the mission I'd given – or perhaps *offered* would be a better word for it – to Talia earlier that evening, wondering how she was getting on. I'd asked her to try and access her father's computer systems, to see if she could come up with any hard evidence against the man, and I hadn't had to ask twice. She was motivated to get back at the man who had given her so little, and was taking so much, and the danger of being caught no longer seemed to phase her. It was as if my presence there lent her a strength that she had previously lacked.

And now – with this surprise night-time hunt, and her father and a large contingent of Vanguard staff out of the house – she had a great opportunity to go through with it.

I prayed that she might have something for me when we returned.

Putting her out of my mind, I turned my attention back to the hunters. They were on a raised hillock right out on the plain, close to a herd of antelope drinking at the edge of a small, winding river which sparkled in the moonlight. Through my scope I could see Garner and Badrock lying on their sniper mats, the general acting as a spotter while Garner aimed through the thermal scope of his own rifle.

The lions which stalked the herd of antelope didn't have access to thermal scopes or high-powered rifles; but then again, they didn't need them. Evolution had equipped them with incredible night vision of their own; and razor-sharp retractable claws, massive canine teeth, and the ability to run at fifty miles per hour and clear almost forty feet in a single bound, meant that they were more than capable of hunting down and killing their chosen prey without any hi-tech equipment.

But the human ability to manufacture weapons to overcome our natural shortcomings was, of course, the reason that we are the apex predator on the planet. Without claws, sharp teeth, strong jaws, speed or endurance, we rely upon technology to see us through; and in the arms race, we have no equal.

Which is why I knew it was only a matter of time before Ian Garner put one of his North Fork 300 grain .375 PP rounds through one of the lionesses that were quietly stalking the antelopes. The cartridge had a small ring cut into the ogive that guaranteed full expansion of the bonded-core soft-point within two inches of penetration, creating an extremely effective kill shot.

It disturbed me somewhat to discover that cartridges were being specially manufactured for the express purpose of taking down big cats, but it didn't surprise me. Human ingenuity was capable of being used for any endeavor. And, I supposed, if people were going to hunt these animals anyway, it was actually better for them if they were killed quickly. Inefficient cartridges would only prolong the agony, the animal limping off to safety before succumbing to its painful wounds, perhaps days later.

I still wasn't sure what I thought of hunting anyway. In a way, it was a part of our human history, encoded in our very DNA. The hunting – and then cooking – of meat had enabled us to evolve shorter guts than our primate cousins, allowing us in turn to use the spare energy to evolve ever larger brains. In a way, hunting animals is what made us who we are today.

But that was to *eat*, to *survive*. I had no problem with cultures or societies that killed things in order to eat them; it made sense to do so. And hunting also made sense if it was used as part of a tactic to limit animal populations, such as the legal hunting of cougar in several US states.

Trophy hunting, however, was something I struggled to come to terms with; especially here, where the animals were supposedly protected, quite often members of an endangered species.

I'd killed my fair share of men, yes; I had even sometimes hunted them down.

But it was never as a trophy. The men I'd killed – and sometimes women too – were dangerous, a threat to others. Terrorists, assassins, the leaders of criminal gangs – they were my targets, and the world was a better place without them.

The animals here were supposed to be protected, to have sanctuary so that their numbers could be rebuilt; it seemed wrong to hunt them, to kill them.

But, I supposed, if I was willing to kill my own fellow human beings – sometimes in cold blood – what right did I have to preach to others?

Kane nuzzled me from the side, and I stroked his warm fur.

That's right, I thought to myself. *Animals are innocent. And some humans aren't.*

Kane's body jerked under my hand as a muffled shot rang out in the still night air, and I saw the thermal signature from Garner's rifle through my sight.

I quickly swept my rifle toward the big cats, praying that a lion had not been hit.

I adjusted the focus, and was relieved to see that the animals were running, along with the antelope as they all reacted to the shot.

But one of the lionesses was moving slowly . . . Too slowly.

"Yeah baby," the spotter to my left breathed lecherously, "that hurt the bitch for sure."

I watched helplessly as she managed to crawl twenty feet from the killing field . . . thirty . . . and then she stopped moving altogether, collapsed to the floor.

I stared through my scope, saw the chest continue to rise and fall; and then, finally, that stopped too.

"It's a kill shot," I heard Badrock announce through my earpiece. "Delta team, approach on foot and confirm. All other teams keep watch."

I confirmed the message with a blip of my radio, then swept my sight back to the raised hillock, saw the two men still in their positions, Garner's rifle still trained on the animal.

I looked again toward the lioness, once so proud and majestic and now just meat, to be sliced up and put on Garner's wall, and felt slightly nauseated by the thought.

"Good fucking shot," the man next to me said admiringly, but I just ignored him; it was safer for him that way.

Two men then emerged from concealed positions

near to the river, and approached the animal. One knelt by its side while the other aimed a shotgun at the big cat's head.

But there was no need — the first man's hand swiping across his own throat in the classic "kill" symbol confirmed that the lioness was dead.

Back on the hillock I saw that Garner was on his feet now, rifle pumping up and down in the air in a victory celebration, stout little legs hopping about in a sick little dance.

"One shot," I could hear him across the plain even from this distance, "one fucking shot! Fuck yeah!"

I watched him through the scope, the reticle sighted directly on his chest.

It took everything I had not to pull the trigger.

CHAPTER SIX

I woke late in the morning; kills were traditionally celebrated in the bar, and after getting back to the ranch at one o'clock, we'd continued drinking until four.

Badrock, knowing that we would be out again that night – and possibly for a lot longer – had told us to get some rest, duties for key security personnel not starting until midday.

Normally, I enjoyed a drink or two – but the company at the in-house bar had been seriously below grade. The Vanguard men still held a major grudge – not only had I beaten up a few of their number, received the promise of a huge paycheck, and slept with the general's beautiful daughter, but now I'd also gone and embarrassed them all in a shooting contest. It had only added insult to injury, and after a few drinks I could tell that the only reason they weren't burying their beer glasses in my face was because doing so would upset their boss.

Ian Garner was also pretty unpleasant, a jumped-up little asshole who thought he was better than everyone else just because he had money. And now he'd bagged himself a lioness, he loved himself even more. If I'd heard the story once last night, I must have heard it a thousand times – and his skill, bravery and manliness only grew with every telling. It was enough to make me want to ram his ruddy little face through the bar's panoramic window, if only so I wouldn't have to listen to it again.

And Roman Badrock – the charismatic man who had so impressed me initially – was now an enemy, pure and simple. Anyone who did what he'd done to his own daughter didn't deserve to be breathing the same oxygen as the rest of us; he was a waste of the planet's resources, pure and simple.

But despite my disgust, appearances had to be maintained and so I remained in the bar for the celebrations with everyone else, knocking back the beers to make the whole thing seem more tolerable.

I was only on six when a pair of park employees wheeled in the dead animal's head, severed from its majestic body and mounted on a rosewood shield. They didn't waste any time around here, I'd give them that.

The whole room had erupted into terrific applause and cheers, and I could have sworn I'd seen a tear in Garner's eye as he hugged Badrock. He'd then picked up the mounted head, gripped both sides of the backing plate, and waltzed around the room with it to the sounds of the Blue Danube. Everyone had fallen around laughing, but the disrespect being shown toward the dead animal had only served to enrage me further.

"You don't find this funny?" Badrock had asked me, eyebrow raised.

"I see you're not laughing either," I'd replied.

"Just because I'm taking his money, doesn't mean I approve of his behavior. But I'm a facilitator, not a moral judge."

"Me neither," I'd said, and that had been that – Badrock had sidled back over to his rich client, and I'd returned to drinking by myself in the corner.

"Pretty sick sonofabitch, isn't he?" said a voice to my side, and I'd turned to see Hatfield sitting there, watching Garner thoughtfully.

"I won't argue with that."

"Put him in a real battle, he'd shit his pants," Hatfield had opined.

"Wouldn't we all?" I'd rejoined.

"Hah! You got that right, my friend. We sure as hell would. But we'd still get the job done, right?" He'd shaken his head at the waltzing Garner with his dead lions-head partner. "Pathetic," he'd spat. "Don't get me wrong, I've got no problem with people killing things, no problem at all. But that?" He'd shaken his head again. "It's not right. Not what men like us need to do. We *understand*. Right?"

"Men like us?"

"*Killers*," Hatfield had said. "When we kill, there's

113

no pleasure. It's just business. If I ever saw one of my men dancing with a corpse on the battlefield, I'd put one right between his eyes and leave him there for the fucking crows."

We'd continued to chat, and it made me smile now to think that this man, who'd been ready to shoot me during our first meeting, was the only person I'd managed to get a decent conversation out of all night.

The smile faded instantly as I rolled over in bed and remembered that I was alone; Talia had been nowhere to be seen last night, and had never come to my room.

I worried that she'd been caught trying to access those computer files, then felt guilty – was I scared for her safety, or for what she might tell her captors about me if she was questioned?

It was possible, however, that she had been sent to Garner's room as his "prize"; a horrifying thought made only slightly more bearable by the fact that he'd consumed so much brandy that he'd almost certainly been incapable of doing anything except sleeping, and snoring loudly.

I checked my watch, saw that it was only just after nine in the morning. I had plenty of time, but I was unaccustomed to lying in so late anyway, and rolled slowly out of bed, padding across the oak floorboards to the open doors which gave way onto a wide verandah with magnificent views of the grasslands and mesas beyond, which rose imperiously into the deep blue sky above. The sun was already getting strong, and Kane was bathing happily in it, in a position unchanged since he'd got back here last night.

I yawned loudly – which drew only a single, rapid check with one eye from Kane – and slowly stretched out my aching body. I wasn't sure that beds agreed with me; after sleeping so many nights out under the stars, perhaps I couldn't tolerate the luxury? I briefly wondered if perhaps it wasn't the bed, but the dozen or so beers I'd consumed that morning, but ignored the thought as soon as it raised its ugly head.

I went back into the room to get myself an espresso from the professional-grade machine on the dresser, then carried it back out to sit with my little buddy.

"How you doing, boy?" I asked as I plunged into a wooden chair by his side, ruffling his hair. My question was rewarded by complete silence and utter disinterest, but I continued petting him anyway. Even if *he* wasn't bothered, I liked it. I sipped slowly at the strong black liquid as I stroked Kane's back, and went through my plan of attack for the day.

We had to report to security headquarters at midday, when Hatfield would give us our briefing. The guests were due to arrive throughout the afternoon, in time to have dinner with Badrock at five. As far as I understood it, I would be responsible for liaising with the armorer to get them equipped, then supervising weapons handling and zeroing on the range. Other people would familiarize them with the park grounds, and general hunting tactics.

I would learn more at the briefing, but right now all I wanted to do was find Talia.

After all, I considered once again as I stood, I didn't have to report in until midday.

There was plenty of time to find her if I got started now.

CHAPTER SEVEN

Midday came around all too quickly, and I'd had no luck in finding Talia. The closest I'd come was a cryptic *she's busy now, you'll get to see her later* from Hatfield; and it hadn't so much been the words, as the strange half-smile on his face that had unnerved me.

But there was work to be done now, and I wanted to do some intelligence gathering of my own; Hatfield was about to tell us who was coming for tonight's hunt.

The Vanguard employees who would be working the hunt tonight – there were about thirty of us, almost a platoon-sized contingent – were gathered in the meeting room of the security base. We were seated on a mixture of easy chairs and sofas, and Hatfield was holding court at the front, stood in front of a lectern with a projector screen behind him.

"You might already know," he began after the

audience settled down, "but tonight's hunt is special, both for the number and the status of the hunters. And maybe some other reasons too," he added with a knowing chuckle that was reciprocated by the Vanguard men.

"That's why we've got the 'A-Team' here, the people we can trust, and why the rest of the permanent park staff have been sent on an all-expenses paid trip to Vegas. And don't worry," he added quickly, before the men could complain, "you'll get to go too. Except you guys will be getting a whole *weekend* there." There were cheers and applause, and Hatfield eventually calmed it down and continued. "We simply cannot afford for things to go wrong, so pay attention. There have been rumors about some of our guests, and now I can confirm them."

He clicked the laptop on the lectern, and a picture of Ian Garner appeared on the large screen behind him. "Mr. Garner, we already know." He clicked another button, and the picture changed to show a forty-something woman in an army uniform, a colonel's rank on her shoulder. "This is Colonel Yvette Williams, a friend of the general's. A lifetime in the army, but she's been in logistics all that time and she's never used her weapon in anger. She wants to change that now, which is why she's here."

Another click, and another image appeared; and this one I recognized. "Billy Johnson," Hatfield announced to stirrings of interest in the audience, "leading quarterback for the Denver Broncos. He's been here before, and knows how we do things."

The next picture came up, a white guy in his fifties, balding head offset by an impeccably tailored suit. "Paul Gustafson," Hatfield said, "the governor of New Mexico." He smiled. "Now you know how the general got his license for this place."

I remembered Ortiz saying how he was going to appeal to the state government about the park, and started to feel a bit sorry for the man; he'd have more luck getting Kane to help him with his daily crossword puzzle.

"Javier Hernandez," Hatfield said next, as a celebrity photo shot came up of an extremely handsome Latino, shoulder length hair bouncing off his muscular shoulders. There were sarcastic *oohs* and *aahs* from the gathered ex-soldiers. "One of the main stars of *Days of Our Lives*. Fed up with his luxury trailer, wants to get his hands dirty."

"And last but by no means least," he continued, clicking a button to show an incredibly beautiful blonde who couldn't have been more than twenty, "we have Paige Lockhart, the number one country singer in the United States." The *oohs* and *aahs* were real now, mixed in with catcalls and whistles of appreciation. "Used to hunt on daddy's ranch as a kid, now wants to get into the real thing. And get this – she's a spokesperson for the WWF *and* the Nature Conservancy." There was much laughter at this irony, but the best I could manage was to fake a smile.

"So there we have it gentlemen, a combined hunt

featuring six very high-profile – perhaps egotistical, certainly demanding – clients, that we simply cannot afford to let down. Security will be at an all-time high, some of these people are targets for paparazzi and we can't take the risk of this hunt being photographed or filmed. Some of Vanguard's best counter-surveillance teams will be escorting these clients here, to make sure they're not followed, and they'll be brought in via the back gate so that our normal park customers don't see them.

"Gates and security fences will be manned at all times while the hunt is happening, to ensure that nobody gets in. Or *out*," he added with a wry smile, to the amusement and whispered comments of the Vanguard men. It confused me, but I forgot it as soon as Hatfield started talking again.

"Each of our hunters will be accompanied by a three-man team, two on close protection and one sniper on overwatch."

Eighteen men in total to help keep these half-dozen prima donna hunters safe, so that they could slaughter endangered animals and put more dollars in the good general's coffers; the other dozen or so would be patrolling the grounds and manning the gates.

Hatfield was right; the last thing anyone would want would be for these people to be caught in the act.

But that was exactly what I intended to do, why I was still here; even without the computer files Talia had been trying to access, I was going to photograph and film these high-flyers shooting their lions and hippos, their leopards and their elephants.

And there was no way the evidence was going to the police, or to any local or state government; it was going straight to the media. And if it turned out that the mainstream media was also complicit, then there were plenty of independent online avenues to pursue.

The images would get out to the public one way or another, and the six rich hunters would be ruined along with Badrock and his park, maybe the whole Vanguard Corporation too.

There were plenty of high-definition recording devices in the armory, optics designed to capture the thrill of the hunt – or record police or military actions to ensure complicity with the rules of engagement. I would just have to "borrow" some of them when I was there later, sorting things out for our guests.

Even without Talia and those computer files, one way or another, Badrock was going down.

"There's been a change of plan," Badrock announced with a smile, catching hold of me outside the conference room. "I need someone with me for the meet and greet, and most of the men here are hardly the type you want as your shop window, if you know what I mean."

Damn. I'd hoped to have an extended afternoon at the armory to give me a chance to pilfer some of those recording goodies. I wondered if Badrock suspected something; if Talia had been caught, had she told him that it was my idea?

But I'd go with the flow; I'd still have a chance to

get a camera when I drew my own weapon later that night. It would be harder, packed as the place would be with Vanguard men, but I could still manage it if I tried.

"Don't worry," Badrock said – picking up on my discomfiture, if not the reason for it, "Miles will see to it that our guests are suitably armed and briefed. They'll go and see him after having a cocktail or two with us."

"Sounds nice," I said.

"Oh, it will be," Badrock enthused. "Now go and get changed. I've had a lounge suit put in your room for you, should fit you just fine."

A lounge suit? Badrock was really pulling out all the stops to impress these people. I tried to remember the last time I'd worn a suit, or tied a tie, and couldn't do it. Was it back in the Rangers? Or maybe even before that?

But an order was an order. "Yes sir," I said. "When and where?"

"The bar at my house," he replied. "Our first guest is arriving within the hour, so shall we say thirteen-thirty?"

I checked my watch, saw that it was quarter to twelve. "Yes sir," I said again. "I'll see you there."

"Excellent," the general said. "And remember – we want to make a good impression. We're counting on you."

The cocktail meet and greet was a pain in the ass.

In addition to me and the general, there was Groban – who, from the looks he gave me, hadn't quite forgiven me for holding the knife to his throat – and a couple of other senior park personnel, along with half a dozen of the better turned-out Vanguard boys. All ex-officers I assumed, from the cut of their suits and the way they drank their champagne with their pinkies sticking out.

Everyone played their role well, kissing ass in exactly the right way to make the clients think they were the real deal. I tried, but didn't do a very good job of it; the people there didn't impress me, and it was hard to pretend.

It was the country singer first, and the officer boys were literally drooling over the girl; and then over the course of the afternoon, the remaining clients arrived, each one more egotistical, more overbearing, and more full of themselves than the one before. And as each new one came in, another was taken out to get their weapons and equipment sorted, until finally there was nobody left but the troops.

The strangest thing about the session was the fact that – despite my refusal to kowtow and bow down to them – they all spent most of their time with me. I was the first one the general introduced, and the one they always drifted back to after doing the rounds. As for why, I wasn't sure. Were they like animals, drawn to the people who didn't make a fuss over them, the ones that seemed inherently more stable, a feeling they could only pick up on subconsciously?

Or was it something else altogether? Something . . . worse?

The whole situation seemed odd – it was almost

like I was being paraded in front of them, for their entertainment. I felt like I was part of a dinner menu, and the guests were hungry.

"Good job everyone," the general said, taking me away from my thoughts. "We've got time now to sort out our own personal weapons and equipment, have a bite to eat, then we're meeting up at the main rendezvous point once the park has been cleared at eighteen hundred. Got it?"

We all agreed, and drifted off to sort out our business.

And the nagging feeling that something was desperately wrong followed me all the way.

CHAPTER EIGHT

The feeling lasted right up to eighteen hundred – or six o'clock, if you prefer – at a site a couple of hundred yards from the front gate.

I had the SCAR back, a secondary thermal recording sight hidden in my sleeve, and a standard daytime mini-camera attached covertly to the front of my combat webbing. Even now – when light conditions were good, before the sun went down – it was filming, recording the famous faces around me.

It had been hard to smuggle the units out under the combined scrutiny of Hatfield, the armorer, and a couple of dozen Vanguard men who were also drawing weapons, but I'd managed it; it was all about distraction and sleight of hand, as any pickpocket will tell you.

The excitement on those faces was palpable, those of the soldiers rather more resigned, perhaps even bored.

Something about the situation bothered me, and I could feel the hackles rising on Kane as he stood next to me, but I decided it could wait as Badrock started to address the sizable crowd.

"Friends," he said, arms open, "thank you for being here this evening, on what I hope will perhaps be our park's most memorable hunt thus far."

There were whoops and calls from the crowd, which died down with a wave of Badrock's hand.

"Yes," he said, "tonight is when hunting becomes *real*."

At this, a commotion erupted from the side of the crowd, and I watched as six men were marched into the open area where Badrock stood. Cheers rang out, but again the general silenced them with his hand.

I recognized the men as workers from the park, four of them Mexican. I wondered if the other two came from backgrounds like Benjamin Hooker, homeless and with nobody to miss them, nobody to ask questions, and finally things started to fall into place and I was horrified that it had taken so long to do so.

I think perhaps I had suspected, but had erased the thoughts, too diabolical to even consider.

But there they were – six park workers, *handcuffed* I could see now, one for each of the hunters. And then I realized what was wrong with the clients, what had been bothering me, what I had picked up on that had made Kane react to my own subconscious reaction.

The weapons the clients were holding were not game rifles – there were no big-bore elephant-killers here.

Just man-stoppers, each and every one perfect for hunting human game.

The fear on the faces of the handcuffed workers indicated that they'd worked out the same thing.

One of them tried to run, but was brought down by a blow to the back of their head from Hatfield's rifle butt, much to the amusement of the crowd.

The graveyard at the old chapel flashed before my eyes, the body of Ben Hooker and so many more – all killed by hunting parties like this.

There had been no "accidents" here.

"Yes," Badrock said, "tonight you will get an opportunity afforded to very few. *Very* few. The chance to hunt man, to kill another human being. Without fear of prison, without moral judgement. Just the thrill of the chase, the ecstasy of the hunt. And I will tell you this," he continued with a gleam in his eye, "once you get a taste for it, you will thirst for nothing else."

The general turned to me then, eyebrows raised. "Does this shock you?" he asked.

I had no idea what to do, the emotions raging through my body uncontrollably, the fear on the faces of the handcuffed men heartbreaking, and contrasting totally with the masks of evil that covered the faces of the baying crowd.

I hefted the weight of my rifle, wondering for a split second if I could kill them all.

But I knew that almost every single person around me was also armed, and I wouldn't stand a chance.

But could I stand by and let this happen?

I breathed out slowly; if I reacted incorrectly now, I was sure to die. I would have a better chance in the field.

"No," I said eventually, "not really. I'd suspected as much."

"And you have no problem with this?" the general probed.

"Why would I? You know my background, you know what I've done. A human life isn't much, in the overall scheme of things."

"Ah," the general said, nodding his head to one of the guards nearby, "but what about *this* human life?"

A second later I could hear the screams of a girl.

Talia.

The soldier reappeared, dragging the general's bound daughter behind him and throwing her at her father's feet, where she collapsed, tears blinding her.

"Son of a bitch!" I yelled before I could stop myself, raising the SCAR reflexively.

The next instant all I could see were stars, as someone gave me the same medicine as Hatfield had given the handcuffed worker, a blow right behind the ear with the heavy butt of a rifle.

Out of the corner of my eye I saw Kane reacting, jaws open wide; then his body spasmed in pain as he was hit by a Taser on full blast, two other men rushing forward, hooking the nooses of their catching poles over my poor friend's neck and drawing them tight.

Kane whimpered, weak from the shock of the Taser, and the men held him still, pinned to the ground with their poles, keeping well away from him.

My rifle was taken away from me and I was dragged to my feet, a man on each side of me.

"Yes," Badrock said, "we caught my little daughter here trying to hack into our systems. With some 'persuasion', she told us that *you'd* asked her to." I didn't want to know what persuasion they'd used, but I didn't blame the girl for talking one bit. Why had I asked her to help me? I'd sealed her fate forever.

"Now why would you want her to do that?" Badrock continued. "A man I'd been good to, a man I'd given a nice, well-paid job to?"

I didn't respond, just stared at the general with hate in my eyes.

"Anyway," he carried on nonchalantly, "she's useless to me now. I can't possibly trust her again. So it's goodbye sweetheart, I'm afraid," he said, looking down on her with mock pity. "It's time for you to pay the piper."

"Son of a bitch," I breathed, eyes still focused with hate on the general.

"Perhaps," he said. "Perhaps. But I haven't even touched on what makes tonight so special, why these people are paying five million *each* to be here." He smiled at me. "They're here for *you*, my friend. The ultimate game. They've come here to see if they can be the one to bring down the Thousand Dollar Man."

CHAPTER NINE

I saw the hungry, sadistic smiles on the faces of the hunters, the smug satisfaction of the Vanguard men, and felt a chill go through my very bones.

Badrock smiled. "You thought I wouldn't find out?" he asked, before shaking his head slowly. "I was always going to find out, you know. *Always*. And we've been having a bit of fun with you, to be honest. The little cocktail party this afternoon was to whet our guests' appetites, so they could get to see the main prize."

The general looked the other handcuffed men up and down with a touch of disdain. "Oh, they have these men to hunt too, of course. *Her* as well," he added as he kicked his daughter with a booted foot. "But I really don't think any of them are going to present too many problems for our guests here, do you?" He laughed. "But you? You're a different story altogether."

He turned to the gathered crowd. "The main event tonight," he announced, "is Colt Ryder, an ex-Ranger, an elite soldier who saw action as part of a specialist recon team in Iraq and Afghanistan. Winner of the Silver Star, the Purple Heart no less than *three* times, *and* the Medal of Honor for his valor in combat. Now known by the *nom de guerre* 'the Thousand Dollar Man', a do-gooder private eye slash bounty hunter slash mercenary who wanders the country helping people sort out their problems, for a thousand dollars a time. This is a man trained in camouflage, concealment, living off the land, silent killing techniques, advanced armed and unarmed combat, demolitions, the list goes on. A man that now kills for money, a man who is *very* good at it. He is not your ordinary prey. He is a legend, a myth, perhaps not a man at all but something altogether more valuable.

"And so one of each of your five million dollar contributions will go to park funds, to help our conservation program." There were subdued laughs and chuckles from the crowd, although it might well have been true. "That buys each of you one of the park workers. You'll each be assigned a territory, and each territory will have one of the workers released into it for you to hunt. But at the same time," he added gleefully, "the Thousand Dollar Man here will be on the loose, somewhere inside the park. A trained killer, an elite soldier, a man who knows the park layout and can use it against you. A hard target if ever there was one. And so the man – or woman – who bags Colt Ryder will win the rest of the money, a total of twenty-four million, as well as getting the right to hang his handsome head from your wall."

There was animated conversation among the hunters and the Vanguard men, as they looked me over like the piece of meat they expected me soon to be.

"But there's an added wrinkle," Badrock said. "This time *I'll* be hunting too; and if *I* get him, then the money – and the glory – is all mine."

He looked across at me. "That okay with you, sweetheart?" he asked with a crooked smile. "You want to play the game?"

I kept my eyes leveled on Badrock's. "It's not a game when the other players don't have a chance."

"Oh," Badrock said as he looked at the helpless park workers, "I wouldn't say they have *no* chance. Sure, they don't have weapons, they don't have infrared, thermal or night vision optics, they're not trained and they have no idea what they're doing, but don't consign them to their graves too quickly. *Everyone* has a chance."

"I wasn't talking about *them*," I said, "I was talking about *you*." I cast my eye over the hunters and the soldiers hired to protect them and let a smile flicker across my features. "You get me into that park and come after me, and you're all going to be *dead*. I swear I'm going to kill every single last one of you."

There must have been something in my eyes – something that told these people on an instinctive level that I wasn't messing around, that I was deadly serious – because they grew suddenly quiet, their false bravado vanishing into the four winds. The hunters kept their smiles pasted to their ignorant faces, but the Vanguard men – those that had seen me in action – knew for sure that I meant every word that I said.

Badrock's laughter broke the silence a few moments later. "Excellent!" he said, applauding me. "Truly excellent! You see, ladies and gentlemen, what dangerous game I have captured for you to hunt! What is a lion, compared to this man?"

The general's words soothed his guests' fears, and their old cockiness returned. "What about *her*?" asked Billy Johnson, the huge NFL quarterback, pointing down at Talia who still lay sobbing at her father's feet.

"Her?" the general asked with disgust. "Consider her a free gift. She'll be released into the park with the others. If you find her, do with her what you will."

Johnson grinned, and I could only imagine what his plans for her would be.

"What do you think of that, Mr. Ryder?" the general asked.

I knew what he was trying to do, of course – manipulate me, goad me into a course of action that he could foresee, and therefore utilize for his own ends. He wanted me to find Talia once we were inside the park; all he had to do was watch the girl and I would turn up sooner or later, the good general waiting for me, waiting to liquidize my skull with a 7.62mm long round.

But I would give the man an answer to his question anyway.

"What do I think?" I asked in turn. "I think that you're a sick sonofabitch. And I think that I'm going to track down little Billy-boy here, and cut off his dick before he does something he regrets. And then I'm going to find you, General Badrock, and I'm gonna shove that quarterback's dick down your throat until you choke on it. And then I might bury your dead body in that little graveyard of yours, along with a sign that reads 'Here lies Roman Badrock, choked to death on a dead man's dick'. How would you like that for your epitaph, fuck-face?"

If manipulation was good enough for the general, it was good enough for me. And for a second, Badrock's face clouded over and I could see that my words had angered him. Generals, retired or not, were not in the habit of having people speak to them in that fashion. But he quickly regained his composure and laughed at my words.

"Well, that's the thrill of the hunt, isn't it?" he said jovially. "Maybe that's exactly what will happen. But then again," he continued, face hard now, "maybe it's *you* who will end up with your dick cut off, my friend. Sliced off and mounted on my wall with my other trophies."

"You'd like that, wouldn't you?" I responded without missing a beat. "Mounted on your wall so you can suck on it whenever you like."

Badrock couldn't even try and disguise his temper now. "You arrogant little fucker," he growled, "you'll regret that little joke."

"Who said it was a joke?"

But the general's face didn't change now, it showed no anger, no engineered joviality; it was just deadpan, devoid of feeling and emotion. "Hatfield," he said, and his servant snapped to attention.

The general pointed at Kane, who was alert now, the shock of the Taser blast having finally worn off. He was emitting a deep rumbling growl, lips back over his bared teeth, the two men pinning him with the poles struggling now to contend with his colossal strength.

"Kill the dog," Badrock ordered. "*Now*."

What happened next occurred in slow motion, the adrenaline dumped into my bloodstream altering my perception of time beyond all measure.

I saw Hatfield smile and unsling his rifle, the SCAR carbine's barrel rising to point toward Kane; and at the same time I saw the gleeful wrath in Badrock's eyes, shining bright like a crazed demon's.

Even as the barrel was rising, I also felt the men on either side of me tensing for action, bodies reacting reflexively to the movement of Hatfield's rifle.

But they didn't tense fast enough, and I stamped down hard on the foot of the man to my left, twisting from his grasp and whipping my elbow backwards into his face with a satisfying *crack*.

At the same time, I launched a low side kick into

the other man's knee, bringing him down instantly; the next moment, I'd pulled him in front of me, wrapped my hands around his neck and yanked hard.

The spine snapped and the body went limp, and then I had the man's falling rifle in my hands; but Hatfield had seen my intentions and thrown himself sideways to avoid my shots. It was good that he'd obviously been warned off killing me before the hunt could begin; it gave me carte blanche to do what I needed.

I released the safety as I moved the rifle around, and snapped off four rapid-fire shots, hitting the men holding the catching poles in the chest, two rounds apiece.

They dropped hard in plumes of spraying blood, and I could see Kane was going to rush to my aid.

"No!" I shouted, firing off two more rounds near his front paws. I appreciated his desire to help, but there were so many guns here that he would almost certainly get hit within seconds and I didn't want that happening to my little buddy. "Go!" I shouted louder now. "Go!"

His head cocked in puzzlement to the side for one moment, and then he was gone, running at full speed past the startled onlookers, dragging the poles that were still hanging from his neck behind him.

I watched him running into the darkness, saw other men raise their rifles and fire off shots at his fleeing form, prayed that they would miss.

But, still trapped in the otherworldly sensation of slow-time, I was already swinging my rifle around to fire off some shots toward Badrock, hoping to embed some rounds in the great man's chest.

But then my entire body convulsed painfully, muscles cramping so hard that I knew I must have been hit with the Taser.

I dropped to my knees, gasping for breath; felt my hands still on the rifle, and tried with all my might to raise it again in the general's direction, muscles rebelling but getting there slowly.

Too slowly.

I felt the surge of electricity hit me again, right against my body, and knew somewhere in the dark recesses of my mind that almost fifty thousand volts were pouring into my nervous system.

And then my eyes closed, and I felt nothing.

CHAPTER TEN

I woke up with a pounding headache, and a dull aching in my muscles.

My head came up and I looked around in an attempt to orient myself. I was in the back of a jeep, wrists and ankles bound loosely; and the jeep was out in the wilderness, under a brightly moonlit night sky.

I wondered how long I'd been out.

"You've been out of it less than an hour," a voice came from the front seat, and I recognized it as the general's. "But the nights come in fast around here." There was a pause, before he added, "Although it's almost daylight with that moon up there."

I couldn't tell if Badrock's voice held disappointment or happiness at the fact, but I could see that he was right. Even without electric lighting, I had no trouble discerning the general's features as he stared at me, his face bathed in a silvery glow.

"Do you think that will make things harder for you, or easier?" he asked, and I paused as I thought.

Good light would mean that I would see my hunters more easily than I would otherwise; but of course, they would also be able to see me, and it would make it all the harder to hide or conceal myself.

But then again, with the thermal imaging and night vision technology these guys would be packing, they'd be able to see me as clear as day anyway.

"Easier," I said.

"Yes," the general agreed. "It will negate our technological advantage, to some small degree at least."

"Might be all the degree I need."

"It might," the general agreed, as he took a lungful of warm night air. "It just might. As I told the others, we've never had a man like you here before."

"You prefer the easy option."

"Do I?" Badrock shook his head. "Don't be so sure. If I liked the easy option, why select you? Why entertain you, why give you a chance? I could have just killed you in your sleep. I could have let Hatfield kill you the first time I saw you."

"So why didn't you?"

"Curiosity, I suppose. Boredom, perhaps. Do you know the kind of people we normally hunt here?" He scoffed. "Men and women like the other six targets tonight, untrained and generally useless. Oh, we get the odd surprise now and again, the occasional drifter with a bit of fight in them. But nobody ever lasts long out here."

"I don't suppose they would, given the fact that their hunters have rifles and night vision, and they have nothing."

"Do you think you don't have a chance?"

"I'm different."

"Exactly," Badrock agreed. "*Exactly*. You're different. You're *better*. An elite soldier, in the prime of life, experienced in combat and highly conditioned. Now, we've had combat vets here before, people we've pulled in from shelters, soldiers who've fallen on hard times, you know the sort. But the trouble is, by the time they've got to that stage, they're a mess – mentally *and* physically. Most are alcoholics or drug-dependent, and their bodies have suffered for it. We get the odd gang-banger in too, boys off the streets. They talk tough, think that because they've fired a Glock or a MAC-10 in the hood, they're the real deal." He shook his head, his skull pallid and eerie in the moonlight. "Within five minutes of being out here, they shit their little pants, every last one of them."

He stretched out, yawned, and turned back to me. "But you can see our problem, of course. We need people who won't be missed – people who are here illegally, for instance, and therefore haven't told anyone where they are, or else people from the homeless shelters, or living on the streets. People who won't be missed," he repeated, almost as if to convince himself.

"Benjamin Hooker was missed," I pointed out.

"Yes, and look what a stroke of luck that was for

me," Badrock said happily. "Because that poor unfortunate boy brought me *you*. Imagine my surprise, my *joy*, when I figured out who you really were. The Thousand Dollar Man. A drifter, a myth, not a real man at all. A loner who nobody would ever miss, because nobody even knows for sure if you really exist. But a top solider nevertheless. And therefore a *challenge*, at long last!"

The general withdrew a large Cuban cigar from his breast pocket and lit it, pulling in a great lungful of scented smoke. "Hmm, that hits the spot," he said contentedly. "Would you care for one?"

I was about to turn him down, when a thought occurred to me. "Yes," I said, and took the cigar from him, slipping it into my own pocket.

"You're not going to smoke it?" he asked.

"Not yet," I replied, aiming once again to unsettle him before the games started for real. "I thought I'd smoke it over your dead body, drop the ashes on your bloody corpse. How does that sound?"

"Unlikely," he answered evenly, obviously resigned to my verbal attacks. "Extremely unlikely, as I think we both know."

"How could you do that to your daughter?" I asked, changing the subject, hoping he might provide me with a hint of her location within his answer.

"I'm a practical man," he answered, "and she was a tool to be used, a resource like any other."

"Dammit, she's your *daughter*," I objected.

"Not anymore," he said, "not after what she did.

142

Oh, I managed to keep her various indiscretions out of the papers of course, but you can never entirely defeat the rumor mill, and word had already spread among my competitors. Proven or not, there was no way the army board would give a fourth star to a man with a *crack whore* for a daughter. That bitch cost me my promotion to full general rank, destroyed my hopes of making it into the halls of the joint chiefs. What she's done here is simply pay me back for what she took from me."

"What she took from you?" I asked incredulously. "What about what *you* took from *her?*"

"What do you mean?"

"I mean her childhood," I said. "Absent father, sent away to boarding school, you think that's what she wanted?"

Badrock shook his head pityingly, as if to a child who didn't understand. "I never wanted her in the first place," he said. "Married late, which was a mistake. Never should have gotten married at all. But it looked good for the promotions boards, you know? More stable, more trustworthy." He shrugged. "Whatever. The bitch was nothing but trouble, a real pain in the ass. And then the dumb whore got pregnant. I tried to love the girl that arrived, but I just couldn't; it was a drain on my emotional resources, and I needed every ounce of energy for my job."

He smiled wryly. "I killed her mother, you know." He nodded his head knowingly, his smile widening. "Yes, I killed her one day when I was back on leave, Talia was in kindergarten. And what kind of stupid

143

fucking name is *Talia*, anyway? I was away on tour when she was born, never had a chance to stop my wife naming her. But anyway," he continued, smoking happily on his cigar, "I digress. Where was I?"

"You were killing your wife."

"Of course I was. So I was at home, and it was the same as always, the woman moaning and whining, *clean this, tidy that, don't put that there*, you know the sort of thing. So one day I just grabbed hold of her and throttled her, wrung her damned scrawny neck until the life bled right out of her, right there on the living room couch. Poured a quart of vodka down her neck, arranged a nice little DUI crash scene. I was sure to burn the thing right out too, make sure the authorities couldn't tell what had really killed her.

"I have to admit, I thought about killing the girl too. But whatever you think of me, I'm not a monster – even *I* couldn't bring myself to kill a child in cold blood. And so I sent her off to boarding school. She never wanted for anything, what more could I do? And then she repays my kindness by becoming a crack addict and selling her body on the streets."

He shook his head, obviously still not able to come to terms with her "betrayal". It was clear that the general was insane, and had been for some time; perhaps had always been. He existed in his own private world, and anyone who questioned it was liable to get hurt, or worse.

"You call killing the girl's mother *kindness*?" I asked in disbelief. I didn't mind questioning his private world;

I was going to get hurt anyway.

"Not killing the girl was kindness," he replied. "Misplaced kindness, as it turned out. But then again," he added, "at least she helped me confirm my suspicions about you."

"That's why you sent her to me."

"Of course," Badrock said. "I didn't believe you really wanted to work for me, I suspected that you were sticking around to poke your nose further into my affairs. But I knew it would be hard to get you to talk – and if my suspicions as to your true identity were verified, I also didn't want you injured. Hence my protection of you during your time here. I wanted you fresh for the hunt. My daughter, on the other hand – her I *could* use for information. I knew if your intentions were not sincere, you would either volunteer them to your pillow partner, or perhaps even try and recruit her to your cause. And then it would be no problem at all to get *her* to talk."

It was my turn to shake my head now. "You really are one sick, sorry bastard."

"Here," he said, throwing me a scrap of cloth that I caught in my handcuffed hands. "Part of her dress, torn by my men." He smiled at my visible reaction. "Keep it as a memento of your time together. It's unlikely you'll ever see her again . . . in one piece at least."

"Son of a bitch," I whispered through gritted teeth, putting the piece of cloth away in a pocket.

"Say what you want," the general said, "but we are similar, you and I, much more so than you probably think."

"We've both got a head, two arms and two legs," I agreed, "and we both piss standing up. But the similarities end right there."

"I think not," the general said. "We both enjoy the thrill of the hunt, do we not? You enjoy your work as the Thousand Dollar Man, of course you do. And why not? You hunt down men like me for your clients, and you love it, you cannot lie to me about it, I see it in your eyes, it's like poison in your veins. You want to kill me so bad you can feel it in the pit of your stomach, can't you? Can't you?"

I *could*; I wanted to kill him so bad it *hurt*. But I stayed quiet.

"Yes," he urged. "Of course you do." He finished his cigar, threw it into the dirt outside the jeep. "You're scared, of course you are; armed men tracking you, wanting to hunt you down and kill you, you wouldn't be human if you weren't. But at the same time, you're excited too, am I right? You'll be free out there, free to do what you do best, free to turn the tables, track the hunters and kill *us* instead. A part of you relishes it, can't wait to get started. Am I right?"

I scoffed, but the fact remained that Badrock *was* right. I was scared, yes; and yet, exactly as he suggested, I literally couldn't wait for the hunt to begin. If it was a choice between sitting here, bound and helpless, or being out there with a chance – however slim – of bringing the fight to Badrock and his set of bastard hunting pals, then it was no choice at all.

He was right.

I was a hunter, and I wanted the game to start.

"You might not be wrong," I allowed. "So when do we begin?"

"Ha," the general laughed, "I knew it. I knew it! Yes, that's the attitude, that's the spirit I've been waiting for all these years. A worthy opponent at last, someone *worth* hunting."

"So let's get on with it then."

"You're right," the general allowed. "The night is not getting any younger." He pointed at the ground outside the jeep, gesturing for me to get out. I did so, putting my bound hands on the side of the jeep and levering my tied ankles over the top, dropping heavily to the dusty floor.

I looked around warily, unsure of what was out there.

"Don't worry about the predators," Badrock said. "Due to the nature of the guests we have here, we've taken the precaution of rounding them up and locking them away for the night, in those pens you saw on your familiarization yesterday. All of them except the crocs anyway, so you might want to stay away from the river. Hippos aren't too friendly either, come to think of it.

"As you've no doubt noticed, your bindings are not tight. You'll be out of them in a minute or two at most, by which stage we'll have driven away from here. But we'll be back, I can assure you. You've got a half hour's grace, to get yourself sorted. Hide, if you can. Come up with some sort of plan, if you want."

He looked up at the moonlit sky. "Beautiful night," he said, "but it's not going to last. A storm's moving in, our first in months. Gonna be a big one, and I couldn't be happier. I *love* hunting in the rain. It just seems *right*, you know?

"You're fair game to any of our hunters, but they're amateurs," the general said. "So try and stay alive until the storm starts at least. Because you know that it's going to be *me* that seals your fate, my boy. I'm going to find you in the rain and put a bullet right between your eyes, and I'm going to fucking love doing it. You hear me? I'm going to fucking *love* it."

"We'll see each other again," I reassured him. "But it's not going to go down like you think."

"We'll see," the general said with a grin, tapping his driver on the shoulder, the jeep pushing up dirt as it pulled in a tight arc around me. "We'll see." The jeep took off across the moonlit grassland, Badrock's lunatic laughter echoing behind it.

As the jeep ploughed on until it was out of sight, I looked at the wilderness around me.

Alone at last.

The hunt had begun.

PART THREE

CHAPTER ONE

I crouched low within the stand of black pine, eyes and ears scanning my environment.

I'd moved just moments after the jeep had disappeared from view, reluctant to stay out in the open; for all I knew, there were people watching me right now.

I didn't kid myself that hiding in the trees would keep me from being detected; thermal imaging would still pick up my heat signature between the trunks. But it still provided cover from fire, and a sniper was less able to put a bullet in me with a thick bit of pine in the way.

The bonds that secured me had – as Badrock predicted – not taken longer than a minute to shed. The thermal imaging, however, was going to be a *real* problem, that much was clear, and I began thinking about ways to defeat it. The problem was, there weren't many. Mylar space blankets could trap heat, but only for a time. The Taliban in Afghanistan had used thick woolen blankets to disguise their heat signature, but again this only worked for short periods; and in any case, I didn't have any blankets to use even if they *did* work. Acetate or glass could also be used to block signals, but the shape would still get picked up and – let's face it – a three-foot by six-foot sheet of glass moving about the New Mexico grasslands might just garner some attention. And like the blankets, I didn't have any glass anyway.

I'd already started to rub dirt over my exposed skin, pulling it up in great handfuls from the ground next to me. It was dry and wouldn't really stick – and probably wouldn't help much anyway – but any camouflage was better than none, and there was no point allowing my pale skin to draw attention in the moonlight. I attached grasses, sticks and leaves to my black uniform too, mud and twigs in my hair to try and break up my outline as best as I could. It might give me a few extra seconds, and that might be all I needed.

Finished with my basic camo, I lay completely still, and absolutely silent, tuning myself in to the world around me. Yes, the moon was bright, and I might see people approaching; but their imagers would pick up my heat signature from a long way out, which meant that the only hope I had to detect any pursuers in the area was sound.

Sound travels a long way, especially at night, and although the Vanguard men might have known what they were doing – although most of them probably didn't – the civilian hunters were bound to have poor noise discipline.

You only really developed the talent when your job involved getting close to enemy soldiers who wanted to kill you, and I doubt any of them had experienced that first-hand.

At first there was nothing, just the sound of insects chirping and moving in the undergrowth; then I caught rustling noises, perhaps a small mammal further into the stand of trees.

Seconds passed, perhaps minutes, and I caught the slow foot pads of a large four legged mammal – or perhaps two or three of them – but they were some distance away, and no threat to me.

It took a while longer for the manmade sounds to reach me – diesel vehicles, voices – and I could tell that they were a long way away.

I couldn't be absolutely sure that I wasn't being observed, but I felt that the chances were good that – for the time being at least – I was alone, as the general had promised.

But I still kept low as I emerged from the trees, my training making me incapable of standing tall and presenting a large, easy target.

There were no clouds at all in the sky, and I wondered if Badrock had been making it up about the storm, just to give me something else to think about; but then I sensed the moisture in the air, and realized he was probably right.

It would be another benefit to me, even more so than the moonlight, and I welcomed it. Fourth generation optics were still pretty good in the rain, but it definitely made their job harder, as rain has the effect of making everything the same temperature. It would also limit the range of the sights, as light scatters off droplets of water.

Good news, all in all.

If I lived long enough to see the storm.

But I fully intended to live that long, and even longer besides; my threats to kill the hunters were not mere bravado, I actually intended to go through with it. It was what drove me, what motivated me, the mental key that would not only help me to survive, but to *thrive* out here in the park.

And so, without waiting a moment longer, I began.

I knew exactly where I was in the park, having familiarized myself with all the relevant maps as well as building a visual memory of the place from my various tours of the grounds.

I was on the open plain near the same spot the dogs had killed that zebra on my first day here, which put me in the northeast sector of the vast ranchland. If I kept heading north for a mile or so, I'd hit the fence line of the property; but of course, I had no intention of trying to escape.

I realized that meant other animals would probably be near – on that initial tour, we'd seen zebra, giraffe and elephant all in this area – but they were not generally nocturnal, and would all probably be holed up until morning somewhere, sleeping and resting.

Hippos were active at night, but I knew they generally confined themselves to the water and it was unlikely I would come across one here.

But I wasn't staying here, I was heading to the water; and I hoped that when I got there, the crocs and hippos would be friendly.

<u>**Chapter Two**</u>

I lay in wait, immobile in the branches of a Piñon tree, watching the men below me.

I'd already heard shots fired from far away – a man's screams, other men's shouts of victory – and I'd known the half-hour was well and truly up, and the hunt had started in earnest.

And the first scalps had already been taken.

Probably the first guy – terrified – had just run in circles, or else not run at all, just stayed where he'd been dropped off, too scared to even move.

Easy pickings for a man with a night scope and an accurate rifle; it was no sport at all.

The second kill had occurred in what I thought must be my sector, a mile or two north, probably near the fence line. It was an obvious enough choice for the victim to have made, an attempt to escape this pit of death.

It hadn't worked.

So that was two sets of hunting parties free to pursue me now, having taken the easy prey first.

I'd heard their vehicles approaching while I'd still been at the river bank, covering myself from head to toe in cool, wet mud. I'd chosen a spot by the river – which was more of a creek, really – which was approachable only via a narrow track through a wide Piñon wood, and made no effort to cover my tracks; even at night, the hunting team should be able to follow them.

It was for concealment, but also because I assumed that crocs and hippos would prefer more open areas of the river; luckily I'd been proved right, and my night-time mud bath hadn't been disturbed by any killer beasts.

I'd then reversed back into the wood, careful to place my feet back into the same tracks I'd made going the other way, and pulled myself quickly up into the tree to wait for the men who I hoped would already be on my trail.

The sooner they arrived, I believed, the safer I would be; for with every passing minute, my heat would build and threaten to emerge through the cool mud I'd caked myself in.

The hunters had arrived quickly, as I'd hoped, and I could hear the jeep idling nearby; the wood had forced them to move in on foot, another reason for my choice of location.

As they passed below me, I saw they were not all

men; the paying customer was Yvette Williams, the army logistics colonel eager to get her first kill.

There were two Vanguard men with her, and I assumed that the third – the overwatch sniper – was probably back with the vehicle, not having had time, or enough information, to set up an effective fire position.

They followed the trail below me in silence, except for the occasional metal-on-metal contact of weapons and equipment which was common among amateurs. Eventually they reached the river, and I heard the colonel's voice.

"Dammit," she said angrily, "there aren't any tracks going back, he must have gone into the river."

"What do you want to do?" asked one of the guards, unconcerned now with noise discipline.

"There's no way we're going in there after him," she said. "Let's get back to the jeep, we'll try and pick up his trail on the other bank somewhere."

I steadied myself now, knowing the moment of truth was nearby – my first, and possibly therefore also my *last*, opportunity to get into the game for real.

I controlled my breathing – in through the nose for four, hold, out through the mouth for four, hold, keep repeating the pattern until calm – and then they were right below me again, far less careful now that they'd designated this trail as safe.

Just as I'd hoped.

As they passed by, I moved within the branches, shifted my bodyweight, and let go.

I dropped to the ground, right behind the rear

marker; I immediately reached forward, just as he was reacting to the noise, grabbed his shoulder with one hand and around his jaw with the other and wrenched violently in opposite directions, snapping his neck and killing him instantly.

I scooped up his rifle and instantly fired it at the second man, who was still only mid-turn, and buried four rounds into his torso.

Within the next second, I'd leaped over his body and was in front of Williams, who had turned her body but failed to raise her rifle at the same time; it still hung uselessly on its sling. The barrel of my rifle, however, was jammed right up underneath her chin; and I saw the terror on her face as her night goggles picked up my frightening, mud- and twig-covered visage, an avenging monster come straight out of hell.

Her throat constricted as she tried to speak, but my trigger finger moved faster, a single high-powered round surging up through her head and blowing the top off her skull, blood and brain erupting, black in the silvery moonlight.

I picked up the body – the lightest of the three – and held it against my own as I stalked back down the trail to the jeep, and the third Vanguard man who was almost certainly now on full alert.

He would fire at the body as we emerged, and I would reply in the direction of the muzzle flash.

But before I got there, I heard growling, and screaming, and tearing and ripping, and I dropped Williams' dead body and edged forward slowly to see what had happened, rifle aimed ahead of me.

I saw the edge of the wood, and an animal padding down the track toward me.

I relaxed; there was no missing that happy, carefree gait.

Kane had found me; done the business on Vanguard man number three as well, saving me the job.

I didn't know how he'd rid himself of those catching poles, but they were nowhere to be seen. I thought back to the dog fighting pit I'd originally rescued him from, and realized that tonight probably hadn't been his first experience of those evil contraptions.

I bent my knees as he reached me, ruffling his head. "Good boy," I whispered, overjoyed to see him. "Good boy." I turned back to the bodies behind me. "Now let's see what goodies we can find, shall we?"

As I've said before, to the victor go the spoils.

CHAPTER THREE

An hour passed, and I'd heard more screams and shouts from around the park; I thought three or four out of the six workers must have been killed by now.

I still hadn't heard Talia, and wondered what had become of her. She hadn't asked for any of this, had been cast out into the wilderness to be hunted down like an animal because I'd asked for her help.

There were no sightings of her reported by the other teams either, at least up until Badrock had realized that I'd stolen a radio and ordered the frequency to be changed. The small device and earpiece were useless for the time being, but I'd already got something out of them, barking out a short, garbled plea for assistance at the wood in the hope that other teams would descend on the area to help.

I had weapons, too – an HK417 assault rifle

160

chambered in 7.62mm, a .40 S&W Sig Sauer P226, a hunting knife with a blackened six-inch blade, along with a nice little multitool and plenty of ammunition. The Vanguard men had also each had a couple of thermal grenades on them, and I was more than happy to add these to my arsenal too.

I'd also taken night vision goggles – the kind that used existing light and intensified it to create the familiar ghostly green image – and a fourth-generation thermal imaging unit. The HK417 also had a TI, the same as the SCAR SSR I'd used the night before.

The kit weighed me down and made me more noticeable, but it was a trade-off I was willing to make. *Never turn down a weapon offered to you* was my motto – whether it was offered willingly or not.

I'd used the preceding hour productively, first setting a little trap back on the woodland trail.

I'd dragged the body of Yvette Williams back to her fallen comrades in the middle of the track, leaving them in open view. Then I'd poured a nice bit of gasoline – from a spare jerry can strapped to the back of the jeep – around the surrounding area, leading it back to the jeep itself, where I'd put the jerry can back where I'd found it.

I'd then put one of the thermal grenades under Williams' body, her jacket attached to the pin by a short cord, and put her back on the ground, face down.

I had then retreated to my present position, halfway up a small ridge about a third of a mile away from the wood, and waited.

But I hadn't forgotten Talia – I'd given Kane the torn slip of the dress the girl had been wearing earlier, the one her father had tauntingly presented me with, let him take the scent, and sent him out to find her. With any luck, he'd lead me back to her when I'd finished up my business here.

My patience was eventually rewarded, as I saw not one but two 4x4 vehicles pull up to the wood.

Two hunting parties, drawn by my false, garbled message on the radio earlier begging for help. I knew Badrock would never fall for the ruse, but I was pretty sure someone would – and now I watched as both Ian Garner and Paul Gustafson arrived on the scene, looking over the ravaged, half-destroyed body left by Kane next to the jeep with what I assumed would be a mix of utter horror, and dread fascination.

They then seemed to argue over who would enter the wood first; they both desperately wanted to be the one to kill the Thousand Dollar Man, and suspected I might still be inside.

Eventually, the Governor of New Mexico appeared to overcome the arguments of the Wall Street banker, and it was Gustafson who took point when they entered the wood. Two men went with him, and Garner and the rest stayed by the vehicles, which they'd parked right next to Williams' jeep.

I wondered if anyone would notice the smell of gasoline, but nobody appeared to; perhaps the coppery stench of the dead, bloodied Vanguard man in the jeep was enough to cover it.

I waited, still and silent, as the party disappeared from view, wondering if my plan would work.

And then I saw a flash of light in the trees, heard the muffled *whump* of the thermal grenade igniting as someone tried to turn Williams' body to identify it; then carried on watching as the trees caught fire around the bodies within, the trail suddenly catching fire too, the line of gasoline racing white-hot back toward the jeep.

The men outside the wood tried to react, but their comprehension was too little, too late – by the time they were moving, the flames had already reached the jeep, its fuel tank, and the extra gasoline in its jerry cans, causing it to explode in a huge fireball that took two more Vanguard men with it.

Garner and the remaining two men were left reeling, running in crazed circles from the flames, hands to their eyes to try and dissipate the pain and shock from the loud explosion.

It was an easy job to take them out with the HK417 and the TI scope. Aim – squeeze – Vanguard man down, head popping open like an overripe watermelon; aim – squeeze – second Vanguard man down, skull half-destroyed by the bullet's impact.

Garner I let scrabble around in the dirt for a while, so he knew how it felt – if only for a short time – to be the hunted.

When I finally took the shot, I considered taking him in the gut, make him suffer a bit more; but in the end I decided that wasn't me. Killing the man was one thing; wanton cruelty was another. And so I took out my third hunter of the evening, swiftly with a clean shot to the head that ended things instantly for the short, bespectacled banker.

I breathed out slowly.

Three hunting parties down, twelve people in total.

Not bad for an evening's work.

I didn't waste any time on guilt; I had already justified my actions to myself earlier, so I didn't have to worry about it now.

The hunters wanted to pay to kill people – *innocent* people, who had done them no harm whatsoever. They were just animals to those rich men and women, like any other.

And the Vanguard men protecting them were complicit with the entire enterprise, and therefore just as guilty, in my opinion. They facilitated the hunting of human beings, and protected those who did it, stacking the odds too far in the hunters' favor.

There was simply nothing to feel guilty about.

I considered repeating my tactics here, just wait for the next group to show up and shoot them all with the HK.

But surely someone, somewhere, was going to start putting the picture together, and I doubted whether I could get away with it again.

If Badrock had any sense whatsoever, he would send men up this ridge to find me, would warn the others away from the wood.

It was time to leave and try my luck elsewhere.

A noise came from behind me and I was about to

turn rapidly, go for my pistol or a knife for the short-range kill, when I recognized Kane's low breathing, and relaxed.

If I moved fast, that movement might give me away to anyone looking toward this ridge, and although I didn't think there was anyone out there, I also knew that it wasn't worth taking the risk and felt relieved I'd managed to stop myself in time.

Kane's nose nuzzled me, and I knew he'd found something.

Talia.

He wanted to take me to Talia.

"Okay," I whispered quietly as I maneuvered slowly to my knees. "Let's go."

I could only pray that she was still alive when we got there.

Chapter Four

The night seemed ever darker as we headed south through the park, but I knew it was just the contrast with the blinding explosions I'd just witnessed; I could still see the horizon lit up in flickering orange in the distance, the fires still burning. In comparison to that, all else was blackness.

Then I realized that it wasn't just the fire; the moon was also in the process of being obscured, clouds moving across them, and I knew the storm that Badrock had promised was on its way. Soon everything would be dark, and the rain would start coming down hard.

Kane set a fast pace and I had to work hard to keep up; pretty soon my sweat was washing the mud right off me, and I knew that my heat signature was going to be coming through as clear as day. The rain couldn't come fast enough.

My own optics were picking up plenty of heat signatures too. We skirted around a herd of zebra, standing but dozy; I wasn't sure if they were awake or not. There were gazelle nearby too, and some of these were more obviously asleep, lying down in the long grass.

We even came within about thirty yards of a gigantic rhino, awake and happily chewing on the grass; but I could see no human heat signatures anywhere.

The rain started to fall then, suddenly and without warning, pelting down in perfectly straight lines like old-fashioned stair-rods and just as hard. One moment the night was still and calm, and the next the very air was electrified. Thunder cracked and, somewhere in the far distance, lightning flashed across the sky.

Eventually, we started to follow an incline, which led toward what looked like a narrow gully, and I heard the noises for the first time and cursed; the sound of the rain had been covering them. They were men's voices; a woman's screams.

I felt the passage of hot air next to me, heard the suppressed *crack* of the bullet instants later; my brain relayed the message that someone was shooting at me, but my body had already responded and I was down on my belt buckle, hugging the dirt.

Dammit.

I was too late; Kane had brought me to the right place, but other people had found her first. Found her, and waited for me.

But where were they?

From the ground I checked left and right and barrel-rolled to a small copse of silver sage, seeking whatever cover I could find.

The round had buzzed past an inch over my right shoulder, and it had come from my diagonal left – possibly from the high ground on the left of the gully.

I looked around for Kane, but he was already gone.

Then my radio crackled to life, and whoever it was had obviously put their own handset back to its original frequency. "Mr. Ryder," came a deep, melodious voice that I recognized as Billy Johnson's. "We have your woman." There was no need for him to confirm it; I could hear her terrified screams over both the radio and the open air. But I didn't reply; best not to give anything away, I decided.

"We're gonna have a high old time with her," his voice came through again, "if you know what I'm sayin'. And you *do* know, right? Yeah," he chuckled, "of course you do, you know this piece of ass real well, don't ya?"

Still I didn't reply, just kept to my cover and scanned the view ahead of me as best I could.

"Tell you what," Johnson continued. "You show yourself, and we'll let the girl go, how about that?"

I didn't believe the man for a second; if I showed myself, he would kill me and then take Talia as his prize, with her father's blessing.

But I didn't know how many people there were in that gully. One hunting party? Two? Or even more? Was Badrock there with them?

I just didn't know, but every second that went by

168

was another second wasted.

What was I going to do?

Screams rang out suddenly again, but this time they weren't from Talia; they were the bloodcurdling screams of a man in extreme pain, coming from my diagonal left, up the side of the gully.

Kane was taking out the sharpshooter.

Once again, my body was responding before conscious thought could interfere with it, and I was up and charging forward, gaining ground while everyone's attention would be on their colleague screaming in agony on the high ground.

I covered ten yards at a sprint, found cover and took it; then darted at an oblique angle another ten yards, pushing it to fifteen before diving for cover again, heat signatures finally showing up on my optics ahead of me; and if I could see them, they could see me, so I forced myself as low as I could go and stayed there, buried in the dirt underneath a thick-trunked Rio Grande Cottonwood.

I could see three men in a clearing up ahead, two of them aiming their rifles up the rise to their friend, looking for a clear shot; the other – and from his massive bulk I could see right away that it was Johnson – stood towering over the small frame of Talia, who cowered on her knees beneath him.

The screaming abruptly stopped and – probably thinking the man up there was dead – the two shooters in the gully unleashed their weapons on full-auto, blasting away at the hillside in the hopes of killing whatever creature had savaged their comrade.

I took the opportunity given to me, taking out both men with shots to center mass, single shots that hit them in the chest and put them down and out, permanently.

I hoped that they'd not hit Kane before I got them. Johnson pulled Talia to her feet, a hunting knife to her throat. I could see that her clothes had been half-torn from her body, and I was glad that we'd arrived when we did. I only hoped that I could convince the man not to use the knife.

"Don't do it," I warned, close enough not to need the radio, although I still needed to shout over the rain.

"Fuck you!" he shouted. "Come and fight me like a man!"

There was little chance of that, I thought as I centered the sight over his right eyebrow, just visible over Talia's head; he was keeping himself low, but he was so much taller than the girl that it was a big effort.

"I'm only gonna count to three!" he shouted again. "Then I cut the bitch's throat!" A pause, then – "One!"

I exhaled slowly, held my breath at the half-way point and squeezed the trigger.

Nothing.

"Two!" Johnson shouted over the hard-pounding rain, which was coming down so fast now that the little hollow my body was lying in was almost full of water.

The rifle had failed to fire, and I immediately checked the ejection port; then stopped myself, knowing I had no time to address the stoppage – *three* would be sounded any moment, along with the sickening sound of a jugular being sliced wide open.

I considered going for the Sig, but a pistol shot at this range, in these conditions, to so small a target was nowhere near a guaranteed hit.

And so I did the only thing I could do, and stood just as Johnson was going to call out the final number, my hands in the air. "Okay," I said. "You win. Let's have it out the old fashioned way."

A big smile broke out over the quarterback's face as he tasted victory – at six foot eight and three hundred pounds, it was unlikely he'd been bested in a fist fight in a *very* long time.

"Throw your other weapons away," he shouted over the din of the storm, and I did as he asked, casting away both the Sig and the hunting knife, along with the night vision goggles.

The gully was dark, lit only by the occasional lightning which showed that Johnson had also thrown away his own goggles; neither of us wanted the impact of them burying into our faces if the other caught us with a good shot.

"Let her go," I shouted, and – close now – I saw the big man hit her on the head with the butt of his knife and cast her away, unconscious.

"I prefer them alive anyway," he said with a grin. "They can tell me how much they like it."

"Throw the knife away," I told him, but he just laughed.

"I never agreed to that," he said, and – just as I

came into range – he launched himself forward, thrusting the long blade toward me.

I sidestepped with barely enough time, tried to lash out at his forward leg with my boot but missed in the dark, spinning wildly in the mud and nearly falling on my ass.

Maybe, I considered, I should have tried to take the shot with the Sig.

We circled each other in the gully, which was starting to fill with water, what had been dry ground – and then mud – now turning to a shallow lake beneath our feet.

It was so dark – except for the lightning that flashed every few seconds – that my only chance was to get even closer to the man. The occasional light only made the dark seem even blacker than before, rendering me all but blind.

But I knew the same would be true for Johnson as well, and – appearing to each other in a lightning flash at about six feet apart – I used the next bout of darkness to race forward through the rainwater.

When the next flash happened, I was suddenly right in front of him, catching him off-guard completely; he swung the knife instinctively but it was careless, and – in the pitch black – I chopped the edge of my hand down toward his forearm, hoping to force him to drop the weapon.

But he must have read my intention, and moved his arm quickly, swiping the blade horizontally across my body; I felt the searing, hot pain of a laceration opening up across my abdomen and prayed that it wasn't deep. My hands shot out to try and disarm him again before I could stop them, and this time he reversed the blade and cut across one of my forearms.

I pulled back reflexively, adrenaline only just blocking the pain, while still knowing that I *had* to disarm the man; and then the lighting flashed as he was coming toward me with a killing stroke, a hard, straight thrust to my chest, and in the darkness that followed I gave over to my training and allowed my body to do what it wanted; and so my own hands shot out to where I calculated his forearm would be and clapped together hard, one hand hitting high near the elbow, the other low by the wrist.

I heard a splash and the metallic *clang* as the knife hit the ground, and when the lightning flashed next, I could see that Johnson was finally unarmed.

In the next moment however, he was on me, having used the dark just as I had – to close the distance – and I felt his bear-like arms encircle me completely, pulling me in until my head was into his chest and his huge strength threatened to break my ribs, perhaps collapse my chest cavity. The pain in my abdomen erupted in earnest now, and I feared that he was going to force my stomach lining out of the cut he'd opened up.

My arms were helpless, pinned to my sides, and I had no leverage to use my knees; everything was so tight that I couldn't move most of my body at all.

My head was free to a small extent though, and I

turned my face to his massive chest and sunk my teeth into his pectoral muscle, biting down hard around a nipple, taking in all the flesh around it and thrashing about wildly.

He screamed in a high-pitched wail and released the hold enough for me to stamp on his foot then kick off in the reverse direction, sending a knee straight up into his groin. He grunted and released his arms even further, then lightning must have lit up my face like a Christmas gift for the man and he unleashed a big right hand that caught me flush on the cheekbone, putting me down hard.

He fell on me in the next instant, using his body weight to crushing effect. He fought like a typical football player – it was rough, without finesse, but damned effective.

His forehead came down hard onto the bridge of my nose, the force of the blow and the weight of his skull – not to mention the assistance of gravity – breaking it instantly, wracking my face with savage, nauseating pain.

He then pushed a massive forearm into my throat, forcing my head down into the pond-sized puddles that had engulfed the narrow gully, the water close to covering my face and drowning me.

But at such close range the darkness was no longer so much of an issue; everything was touch at this distance, and one of my hands instantly trapped down on the arm that was choking me, my other arm underhooking him on the opposite side. At the same time, my right foot fed onto the inside of his left thigh as my left foot trapped his right and I initiated a roll.

Trapped as he was on one side, he was forced to go with the rapid motion, and then our places were reversed, me on top now and instantly repaying the head-butt, now *his* nose exploding across his face, gravity assisting me as it had Johnson just moments before.

He tried to throw me off with brute strength, but I had already secured my legs in a grapevine hold on his own, pressing my weight down through my hips and spreading him out, keeping him pinned securely. I let my head come down hard a second time, and with the next lightning flash I could see that he was dazed at last.

He tried to punch upward at me, but the blows lacked power and I let my own fists rain down on him, until he tried to turn away from the pain.

I instantly released my hold – just a little – to allow him to escape, to roll onto his front to get away from the punches to his unprotected face, and then re-secured my position, this time mounting from the back.

He tried to buck me off again, but I held him tight and my hands went straight for the neck. He responded by pulling his chin in tight to his chest to protect his throat, but that put his mouth and nose under the water of the rapidly rising gully-stream, and he soon pulled his head back up.

No sooner had he done so than my forearm snaked quickly around his neck, throat in the crook of my elbow, biceps and forearm tight across his carotid artery and jugular vein to cut off the blood supply to the brain, hand clamping itself to my other bicep as that arm fed around the back of his head, and increasing the pressure by leaning my own head onto it, everything so tight now that the hold was literally unbreakable.

The pain in my arm from the earlier cut was intense, the pressure of the strangle forcing blood to pump out of the wound, black in the lightning, but as Johnson's body started to relax, I knew it wouldn't last much longer.

Even with a neck as thickly muscled as Johnson's, unconsciousness came over him in ten seconds; but still I kept the blood-choke on, starving his brain of oxygen; and with his face in the water too, death came only a few more seconds later, and I felt the warmth against the front of my pants as his bowels let go in his final release, life leaving him completely.

Four hunters down.

I sagged, exhausted, onto the big man's back, wanting only to give into the desire to rest, to *sleep*, but I knew that if I gave into that desire, I would be dead soon after; the other teams had surely been informed about Johnson's plans, and would be on their way here now.

Perhaps even *were* here, watching our little fight to the death for their own sick amusement.

The thought made me move, fast.

Rolling off the big man's body, I was up and running for the nearside of the gully, diving into a thicket of bushes I'd spotted during the last lightning flash.

No bullets chased me there, but I couldn't be sure that nobody was watching me.

I saw Talia's body then, unconscious and threatening to be swept away by the violently swirling rainwaters, and knew I had to act, had to throw myself back into open view to get her.

I breathed deep, and accepted the fact that I would soon know if there were armed people watching me.

I would feel the impact of the shot.

I would know.

And then I would be dead.

But what could I do?

I ran anyway.

Chapter Five

The water was coming faster than I'd realized, gushing down the old riverbed with real force now; as I reached Talia, her body had already started to get washed downstream and I almost lost sight of her in the dark.

But then the lightning flashed again and I caught sight of her, waded fast to catch up and finally got a hold of her. I pulled her free of the water, threw her across my shoulders and headed for the nearest side of the raging gully, keeping her secured to me with one hand while I used the other to grab hold of the branches of a tree to pull ourselves free from the mire.

Eventually we were out, legs clear of the rising water, and I continued to pull ourselves further and further up the slope until we were well and truly safe. I looked back down and saw the once dry gully was now a surging torrent of rainwater, taking everything with it –

the dead bodies, the weapons and the equipment.

I lay Talia on her back on the wet slope and checked her pulse, her breathing; she was still alive, although badly concussed from the blow with the knife hilt.

"Colt . . ." she whispered weakly, eyes still half-closed.

"It's me," I told her, careful to keep my voice low despite the noise of the storm. "You're okay. You're going to be okay." I smoothed her wet hair back over her forehead, and in the next flash of light I saw her smiling weakly.

Kane arrived soon after, his muzzle coated with dark blood, and I rubbed his head. "Thanks," I whispered. "Good work, boy."

I heard the noises then, even over the storm – vehicles, engines straining through the bad conditions. Heading here.

I wondered how many there were, if Badrock had decided to call in all hands to help defeat me.

The six workers would be dead by now, I realized, probably even before the rains had started in earnest.

Two hunting parties were left – the pretty little country singer, and the handsome TV soap star – along with Badrock, Hatfield, and the dozen or so other Vanguard men assigned perimeter guard duty. If they were all called in, there would be over twenty of them.

Twenty-to-one weren't my favorite kind of odds.

On the other hand, though, if they were all gathered in one place, it might make killing them all the easier.

That's right, I told myself. *Think positive.*

I remembered reading somewhere once that the man who thinks he *can*, and the man who thinks he *can't*, are both right.

Success was all in the mind.

So fuck the odds.

I was going to kill them all anyway.

They wouldn't see us in these conditions unless they got very lucky indeed, I was pretty sure of *that*. But from my covered position in the tree line of a steep slope, I could see *them* just fine, at least when the lightning hit.

It was as I suspected, Badrock had called everyone together to launch a concentrated attack on me. He'd be panicking now, four of his high-paying celebrities dead and gone, a dozen of his most trusted Vanguard men along with them.

They must have thought that I was still armed, because they'd parked their vehicles in a tight, protective circle and met in the middle, crouched low with sharpshooters posted at the four points of the compass – no doubt ordered to fire at wherever they saw a muzzle flash.

The only trouble was that I *wasn't* armed, and I couldn't really see a hell of a lot either.

I also had the added baggage of Talia to think about.

I needed a place to make my stand, somewhere that Talia would be safe, and that would give me the advantage, even without weapons and equipment.

I thought back to my tours of the park, my study of its maps and plans, and eventually an idea started to form in my mind's eye.

Yes.

I knew where we had to go.

Chapter Six

It had taken me a long time – time in which I was often terrified, sure that my location was going to be observed at any moment – but everything was as ready as it could be, and now all I could do was wait silently inside my dark pit, unable to know what was going on around me.

Unable to know how long I would have to wait.

Talia was safe though, at least; she was at the top of the nearby mesa which towered over us, hidden in a small copse of low bushes. The climb had been hard, and it was unlikely that anyone would bother trying to access the summit.

Back down here, below ground level, drowning was a threat – despite the pit being covered, water was still seeping through and was already up to my navel; before long, I would be forced to escape and the trap would be ruined.

But then I heard footsteps nearby, voices whispering softly, and I knew that at least some of my hunters had taken the bait and entered the graveyard, following tracks that led toward a stand of trees on the far side of the chapel site.

I knew that others would be watching the area, but – for now at least – that didn't matter.

I just had to wait a little longer.

The first scream occurred just a few seconds later, a cry of shock as the ground gave way beneath one of the men, a second cry of pain as their body became impaled on the sharpened sticks I'd placed in the cemetery's open graves, before covering them with branches and foliage so the holes couldn't be seen. I'd sharpened the sticks with the blade of the multitool that had still been in my pocket, and the sticks had in turn also been dipped in animal dung, Vietcong-style, to poison their victims' bloodstreams if the penetration didn't kill them immediately.

There was an explosion next, and I knew that someone – and maybe more than one person – had entered the chapel, where I'd rigged one of my thermal grenades to go off, the only bits of kit I'd retained during the fight with Johnson.

More screams were heard next – more people falling in the pits – and then the covering of my own grave tore violently open and a man fell down, screaming as his chest, leg and face were impaled on my Punji-sticks; in the lightning I saw the eyes opened wide in shocked disbelief, the sharp end of one of the sticks poking through the cheek of his handsome face.

Javier Hernandez.

I was up and moving in the next instant, keen to capitalize on the chaos and confusion that would be erupting around the chapel.

I took the soap star's rifle from his dead hands and rose up out of the grave, scanning the area quickly, lit now as it was by flames from the chapel building.

I saw two flaming bodies through the windows, and another crashed back out of the door, still screaming wildly; I turned away and saw three people still standing in the graveyard, terrified to take another step lest they too tumble into one of the makeshift Punji-pits.

I aimed Hernandez's rifle and shot them all where they stood, drilling them with the high-powered rounds.

I was out of the flooded grave soon after the last man fell, running through the graveyard for the tree line that I had supposedly been hiding in anyway.

I heard muffled shots follow me, felt the hot spray of mud as rounds hit close by, and knew that other hunters were near, watching and observing; but I was moving too fast and the scene was too chaotic, and their bullets never touched me. I was through into the wood, keeping the speed up as I raced toward the far side.

But before I reached the end – which my enemies might have staked out – I broke off through the undergrowth, using a small trail I'd hacked out earlier that night.

I crawled through the small route in the dark, rifle

in my hands, and came out in a small thicket that bordered my next specially prepared location.

I'd left a couple of more surprises back on the woodland trail though, and not a great deal of time went by before more screams could be heard above the torrential downpour, the cracks of thunder, and the rustling flames of the burning chapel.

On either side of my little escape route I'd placed tightly wound saplings, primed to lash back into their natural position when small ankle-high tripwires were hit.

The saplings would have whipped back along the horizontal at terrific speed, burying the spikes I'd inserted into their length right into my pursuers' bodies.

I hadn't actually learned that trap in the Rangers – I'd seen Stallone do it in the movie *First Blood*. But whereas the Rambo character had placed the wicked spikes at leg height so he wouldn't kill the person, I had no such qualms. These weren't innocent cops on my tail, they were hired killers.

I had therefore placed the saplings at about my own chest height; allowing for variance in size, they would hit people anywhere from the gut up to the neck. Even if my pursuers were bent low, they would take the spikes in the face instead.

I had no way of knowing how many were hurt or killed, but I did know that – however many it was – it would sure as hell slow the rest of them down as they worried about what other hellish traps I had laid for them.

They were right to worry, I told myself with a smile as I maneuvered myself into position.

"Hellish" was a good word for what was going to happen to them next.

<u>CHAPTER SEVEN</u>

They were more cautious now, and who could blame them?

I watched as they approached from the east; they knew that I was somewhere beyond the pens, but not the exact location. They could see my tracks though and – although they could no longer be sure if they were being led into another trap – they had no real choice except to follow them, if they wanted to have a chance of killing me.

And killing me, after all, was exactly what they were there for in the first place.

To allay their suspicions, I'd not been quite so obvious with this trail. I'd doubled back, crossed my tracks, brushed some of them away, crept through the underbrush and crossed several rain-swept streams. The trail was genuinely hard to follow, and I'd even worried that – with the storm – they might not actually be able to follow it.

But eventually – with the dawn not too far away now – they came, patrolling slowly and carefully toward a concealed service track which held a series of animal pens, situated purposefully out of the eye of the daytime tourists.

Through the rifle sight I could see that Paige Lockhart, the sole remaining hunter and hypocritical spokesperson for the WWF and the Nature Conservancy, was in the middle of the squad as they reached the service track, presumably for added protection. Badrock probably wanted at least one of them to live.

I wondered if she still even wanted to be here. Surely she was frightened? All of the others were dead now, and that fact surely couldn't have been concealed from her?

And yet she didn't look frightened at all; instead, she looked to be taking charge of the remaining men who – after my special surprise back at the chapel – now numbered less than a dozen.

She gestured for four of the men to skirt around the back of the animal pens and the hillock which concealed them, to investigate the far side of the service track, presumably to see if the trail could be picked up on the far side without having to pass this tactically dangerous area.

But they wouldn't find anything; on the opposite

side of the service track to the hillock, there were numerous other tracks that I could have taken through a wood which followed a steep incline toward the higher ground that eventually led to the mesa beyond, and they would be forced into going that way if they were going to continue their pursuit.

Soon the men returned, and told Lockhart what they had found – open land on the other side, and no tracks. I could imagine their words – *If we want him, we're going to have to go in and get him.*

As they spoke heatedly about their plan, I couldn't help but wonder where Badrock was. Hatfield too. What were they up to? Why weren't they with Lockhart?

But then the squad below me started to move, and my concentration went back to the scene in front of me; Lockhart was ordering her men forward, and another four did as she asked, almost tiptoeing onto the suspicious service track, looking about them in every direction for trip wires, traps and bombs. They were paranoid, and with good reason; they'd seen plenty of their friends killed tonight already, and they surely had no desire to be next.

I watched and waited as they traipsed down the soaking dirt trail, trying to pick up any sign of where I'd gone.

Most of the pens down this alleyway were empty, but two of them were decidedly not, and the men gave these a very wide berth, although they were securely locked.

They scoured the trees to the opposite side with

extreme care, rifles always up and at the ready.

It must have been fifteen minutes later that they finally discovered my false route through the tree line and signaled for the others to come.

Paige Lockhart, relieved that the area was safe, led the others forward into the service area, her own rifle slung casually at her side, supremely confident.

Stupid, really.

I waited until everyone was inside the narrow alley, and then gave a short, sharp whistle.

At my command, Kane broke from his cover behind a large boulder and sprinted forward toward my false trail up into the wooded slope, the long vines I'd tied around his legs pulling taut as he ran.

As the first two lines reached maximum extension, they pulled the pins from the thermal grenades I'd hidden – obviously effectively, given that the search teams had failed to find them – in the undergrowth at either end of the service track.

The grenades exploded with terrific force, white-hot flame cutting off the party's main exits and sending everyone into sheer panic, screaming and shouting and waving their rifles around uselessly.

Kane carried on running and then the next two lines pulled taut and yanked open the restraining bolts of the two occupied cages behind Lockhart and the hunting crew.

Frightened by the flames, and activated into naked aggression by the chaotic scene in front of them, the African wild dogs leaped from their pens and attacked everything that stood in the way between them and the tree line.

The vines were still attached to the locks, but I wasn't worried about Kane – he could easily chew through the vegetation and be free in not more than a couple of minutes.

As the dogs ran wild, some were killed by frantic rifle shots, but still others managed to take their targets down, teeth and claws working frantically and feverishly in the terrible orange firelight to separate skin from bone, muscle from tendon.

Everywhere I looked, Vanguard men were falling, screaming, under the wild onslaught, and Paige Lockhart, country-singing sweetheart and would-be killer, also fell, rifle forgotten now as her hands covered her head, desperate to protect herself from the savage dogs; but there were too many of them and, despite her vain efforts to save herself, she was picked apart and ripped to pieces.

The dogs were wild, crazed into savage ferocity by the flames which licked at the nearby trees, gutting and eviscerating the poor unfortunates who rolled pityingly across the muddy ground in a gory scene of spraying blood, torn flesh and mangled tissue. I saw two Vanguard men who had managed to escape the grenades and the dogs run for the trees, making no attempt to help their fallen comrades, and I aimed my rifle at them and loosed off two shots, one to the fleeing head of each man.

The heads burst open just fractions of a second

apart from each other and the bodies fell, lifeless, to the ground.

The soil next to me erupted just an instant later as a round struck the dirt only inches from my shoulder, and I jerked away reflexively, rolling desperately for a change of cover, praying that a second shot wouldn't hit me.

I rolled behind a slab of rock, my back to the hard protective surface and my heartbeat racing at two hundred beats a minute.

Damn!

It had to be Badrock – probably with Hatfield as his spotter – and I cursed myself for taking out the two last Vanguard soldiers and revealing myself with the rifle's muzzle blast.

That's why Badrock hadn't been with the others – he'd known the service track was the perfect place for an ambush, and had positioned himself to take advantage of it. He'd have seen that I'd taken the rifle from Hernandez, known for sure that I was armed, and understood that I would be lying in wait to pick people off down in the alley.

He would have had a good idea of where I might be, based on his own judgment of angles and effective fire, but not the precise location; he would therefore have positioned himself somewhere that he would be able to respond to my shots when they inevitably came.

It had almost worked too, and I cursed my stupidity; I should have realized the general would have thought of that, and left my rifle alone.

Was I really so keen to kill everyone that I'd been

willing to endanger myself?

Perhaps I was, I could admit to myself; but was it really such a sin, if they were all bad?

Badrock himself had been happy to sacrifice his own people to get to me; he could have warned them away from the trap, but he chose not to, chose to use them so that he could get my trophy head on his wall.

Now *that* was a sin.

And I would make sure that the general was going to be punished for it.

CHAPTER EIGHT

I was back up on the table-top mesa, once more lying in wait for my pursuers.

The night was finally dissipating, the first faint rays of the sun playing at the horizon's edge; but although the thunder and lightning had abated, the rains continued to fall as heavily as ever.

I was lying prone on the ground, using a large rock for cover and pointing Hernandez's German PSG1 sniper rifle toward the only viable route up the mountain.

There was another way up from the rear, but a gully had opened up near the bottom on that side of the mesa which some buffalo had drowned in and was now festooned with feasting, twenty-foot long Nile crocodiles. Besides which, I'd also set a variety of booby-traps across the flat top of the mesa just in case anyone was crazy enough to make the climb up that way.

Talia was conscious now, but terrified and something of a nervous wreck. It was hardly without reason, but I was afraid that her sobbing would give her away and considered knocking her unconscious once again, purely for her own safety. But then Kane had returned, and his presence seemed to reassure her, so I placed him with her back within the bushes while I waited to make my two last kills of the night.

Miles Hatfield.

Roman Badrock.

They were coming for me now, I could feel it in my bones; the general was right, he wasn't a coward, he wasn't the type of man to back down from a fight. I might have singlehandedly taken out an entire contingent of professional ex-military mercenaries and a handful of blood-crazed amateur manhunters, but Badrock probably just saw this as a glorious challenge; when he put my head on that trophy wall, it would be the finest prize of his long career.

Only it wasn't *my* head that was going to end up on that wall.

I don't know how long passed before I heard the near-silent sounds of someone coming slowly up the cliff path ahead of me – I hadn't dared look at my watch for fear of missing something – but the sunrise was nearly here, the blackness of night giving way to the dull grey of a pre-dawn twilight.

Whoever it was, they were moving slowly,

cautiously, and I couldn't blame them for a second; they were moving toward what could be their death.

A few more moments passed, and I went through my regular breathing routine, taking my heart rate way down, ready to make the kill shot the moment I saw my target appear.

A few moments more, and then something rose up into my rifle sight.

Miles Hatfield, ex-Delta commando and right-hand man of General Badrock, a comped-up old-school AR15 assault rifle in his hands, up and ready in the aim.

My finger started to squeeze, then stopped as my body was wracked by a hideous, paralyzing pain that was so brutal, so sudden, I thought my heart would stop right then.

I'd been shot, I knew that much as my wounded body sank into the mulch below me, pain localizing now in the back of my shoulder.

But how?

By who?

Despite the pain, I turned on my ass, back to the rock to cover myself from Hatfield – for now at least – and opened fire across the mesa toward the figure of Roman Badrock, ignoring the pain to make my fingers work the trigger, pumping shot after shot toward him until the twenty round box was almost empty.

I saw the figure run and jump for cover, and as he ran, I knew he must have braved the crocs, come up the hard way to surprise me from behind while his loyal servant took the obvious – and much more dangerous –

route to the front.

I felt stone chips spark off the big rock next, as Hatfield opened fire with the AR15, keeping me pinned down on Badrock's side, open for another shot when the general could reestablish a fire position.

My brain was racing as I considered my options, and then I could see a low, powerful four-legged figure sprinting across the mesa top toward me, past me; *Kane*, moving faster than I'd ever seen him, leaping over the rock with teeth bared.

I heard shots next, screams, violent yells and the savage ripping and tearing of flesh and sinew.

With Hatfield occupied, I rolled painfully around to his side of the big rock, putting the hard cover now between me and the general.

To my surprise, Kane was struggling with Hatfield; the man was still alive, able to fend off Kane's normally unnatural strength, keeping his teeth and claws at bay. I soon saw why – my boy had been shot by the Delta man, taken a 5.56 round through the body, and his fur was matted with his own blood.

Hatfield had dropped the rifle, but I watched as he withdrew a knife and thrust it toward Kane's heavy-breathing chest.

The bullet that I fired without conscious thought caught Hatfield just above the right eyebrow, the bullet driving through the ex-soldier's skull and blasting the back of his head off in an horrific yet perversely satisfying fountain of blood, bone and brain tissue.

Kane fell with him to the ground, weak and

breathing hard; I wanted to run to his side to check on him, but dared not move from my position. Badrock was still out there somewhere, waiting for just a little glimpse of me.

It would be all he would need.

"Colt!" I heard him call out through the storm, and I fingered my rain-slicked rifle, trying my best to ignore the pain that raced from my shoulder and through my entire body, the pain that told me to surrender, to give up, to lie in the muddy pool below me and wait for death.

Another part of me though – a stronger part, a better part – told me to hang on, to not give up, told me that there was still a chance.

There was still a chance.

"Colt!" the voice came again. "I've got your woman!"

Talia.

Dammit, she'd probably run out of cover after Kane; and without him protecting her, she'd have been easy pickings for her father.

I staggered to my feet and swung around into the clearing beyond, free now from cover, my rifle up and aimed as best as I could in my condition, barrel pointed true toward the two people ahead of me.

Badrock had one arm around Talia's slim neck, a .357 Magnum revolver in his other hand pressed hard against her temple. I noted the rifle slung from his shoulder, and wondered – through the mind-numbing pain – what exactly he had planned.

"So here we stand," he shouted across the soaking table-topped mesa, "face to face and man to man at last. Just the two of us left, just as it should be. It's perfect!" he shrieked, and I could see that the sonofabitch was actually *enjoying* this.

I was trying to find a target through my scope, but Badrock was too much of a pro for this and continually changed the angle of both his body and hers, so that I was never presented with a clear shot. In my state, weakened by the gunshot, I would be just as likely to hit Talia as the general.

"I'll tell you what we're going to do," he shouted. "You're going to put that rifle down, and I'm going to release my daughter. Then I'm going to try and shoot you with this Smith and Wesson. It's long range, the conditions are bad, and I only have six shots. You can move too, however you want. You *do* have a chance. When I run out of bullets, I'm going to go for my rifle; and with *that*, I'll hit you no problem. Your only chance will be to try and get near to me while I'm firing the revolver, rush me when the six shots are gone, before I can get my rifle, and kill me with your bare hands."

Well, what did you know? Maybe he was a sportsman after all, I joked grimly to myself.

Badrock smiled. "Think you can do it?"

But there was no thinking; I was already moving, rifle in the dirt as my legs pumped hard, eyes keen on the man ahead of me.

He did as he promised, threw Talia down to the ground, took a double handed grip on the revolver, and fired.

But as he'd said, hitting a moving target in these conditions was hard; not impossible, but *hard*, and it gave me a chance. I was also very aware of where the general was standing, and *that* gave me a plan.

The first four shots went well wide of the mark, the fifth grazing my shoulder and making me momentarily lose focus; but then it was back, and I sprinted the last few yards to my final destination, right at the edge of the mesa cliff-side, where Badrock must have climbed up earlier.

"You're no closer," he shouted happily, adjusting his aim for the final Magnum shot.

"No," I shouted back, "but you are!"

He smiled widely. "If you're talking about that same trick with the sapling you used on my men," he said as he stepped wide around the trip wire that would have set off my trap, "then you're wasting your time." His new position set, he fired off his last .357 round. I moved reflexively, but he didn't really intend it to hit; it was just to cover him as he dropped the revolver and transitioned to the far more accurate hunting rifle that was slung over his shoulder.

I had less than a couple of seconds until Badrock had cleared the rifle and taken aim, but it was all I needed.

My hands reached out for the wooden lever that I'd earlier jammed between the earth and the bottom of a quarter-ton boulder perched on the cliff edge.

It was a superhuman effort but – by sinking all my

bodyweight into it – the wooden lever did its job, and upended the giant rock, sending it tipping over the cliff edge.

Badrock's eyes, halfway up to his rifle sight, went wide as realization dawned. "No," he said, before screaming the word, "No!"

The vine attached to the big rock was pulled tight as the boulder fell fast to the creek below, and the loop that Badrock was standing within – that he'd stepped into when he thought he'd cleverly avoided the obvious, *decoy*, booby trap – cinched fast around his ankles, drawing taut and pulling him to the ground.

But he was fast to react, and dropped the rifle and reached out to grab hold of his daughter's hair, dragging her down with him as the boulder pulled him toward the edge of the mesa.

Now it was my turn to shout, "No!" as Talia was pulled inexorably toward her death.

The weight of the boulder pulled the general fast, ripping him painfully across the mesa's rocky surface, and by the time he reached me he was a bloody mess; and yet as the rock pulled him over the edge, his eyes still registered victory as he kept his grip on the girl, dragging her with him.

But then I was there, my hands wrapped around Talia's and pulling her back, and for a second the general was caught between the two forces, me and the rock; but my grip on her hands proved to be stronger than his hold on her hair, and the weight of the crashing boulder proved too great, and his eyes went wide in disbelief, in horror and fear as his hand let go, Talia fell into my arms, and he fell plummeting down the near-sheer cliff face of the mesa.

I scurried forward to the edge, watching him bounce off the rocky walls all the way down, eyes still wide with disbelief as his bones shattered, his skin ripped, and his organs were crushed to jelly.

The boulder hit first, crashing into the creek in a huge geyser of rainwater, and then Badrock's body slammed hard onto the top of the boulder before sliding, broken and bloody, into the black waters of the creek beyond.

I watched, exhausted and yet unable to take my eyes from the spectacle, as the twenty-foot crocs – evidently tired now of buffalo – swam swiftly toward the general's twitching body, chomping down on him with their massive jaws and breaking him into chunks of bloody meat, turning and tumbling with his parts sticking out of their full mouths in their characteristic and savagely joyful death rolls, before swimming away with the pieces.

I guess I was never going to get the chance to mount his head on that trophy wall of his.

"Good riddance, you son of a *bitch*," I heard a ragged whisper sound next to me, and I turned to see that Talia Badrock had watched the whole thing, the horror of her father's demise not turning her stomach, but rather providing a most satisfying form of closure.

I looked at the girl's beaten, bloody and bedraggled body, glad she was alive.

At least I'd managed to do *something* right.

But my own painful and exhausted body sagged as I looked down from the high mesa.

"Shit," I said unhappily.

"What's wrong?" Talia asked. "We won, right?"

"Yeah," I said in resignation, "we won."

"So what is it then?"

"What is it?" I asked wearily. "It's that now we've got to climb all the way back down this huge fucking mountain."

I smiled through the pain and listened to Talia's laughter, the warm human sound a welcome salve on my war-ravaged heart.

EPILOGUE

I spoke to Kayden from a payphone in a coffee shop just off the Las Vegas Strip.

I wouldn't normally travel so far in one go, but I figured that killing the Governor of New Mexico – among several notable others – would probably cross me off some people's Christmas lists.

I actually had no idea if any law enforcement agency was looking for me – the "incident at Badrock Park", as the popular press referred to it, had been described as an horrific accident, all the people killed supposedly having been enjoying a party in the main house when a gas main blew and incinerated the property, along with everyone in it.

It was obviously a cover-up, and if Badrock's connections ran as deep as I suspected, then it shouldn't have surprised me at all. He'd served some powerful people over the years, and none of them would want the truth to be revealed.

Talia had wanted to go to the press with the computer files she'd found, but I advised against it – she wouldn't know who to trust, and approaching the wrong people could easily get her killed.

Back at the ranch, all those days ago, I'd got her to patch me up in the headquarters medical room as best she could; without painkillers to dull me, I'd guided her through the process of removing the bullet from my shoulder, then got her to clean the wound and sew me up.

She was a good student, but I took care of the other injuries myself. The knife wound to my stomach was painful but superficial, while the slash to my forearm cut deeper and needed quite a few stitches. The damage to my other shoulder where the bullet had grazed me wasn't too bad, and everything else was just cuts and bruises that weren't anything to get excited about; it was nothing that a bit of rest and relaxation wouldn't sort out.

I was more concerned about Kane though, my little buddy that had thrown himself on Hatfield to protect me and taken a shot in the belly for his trouble.

Despite my own condition, I'd carried him off that mountain myself, doused him with painkillers and removed the bullet before I'd allowed Talia to touch me. And whereas I was reluctant to seek medical attention for myself, there was no way I was going to apply those same principles to Kane; and so I had Talia call an emergency vet even as I was patching myself up.

The guy hadn't asked too many questions, despite the seriously bedraggled state that Talia and I were in, and had commended me on doing a good job of removing the bullet. Apparently, Hatfield's shot had missed the major organs, and was unlikely to prove fatal. With a complete medical facility to use, he put Kane on a drip and dosed him up with a serious combination of high-powered drugs.

With Kane alive and blissfully out of it, the vet had turned his tender ministrations on me; he could tell that I'd been shot, and assured me that humans were just another sort of animal to him. He'd tidied up Talia's stitching and given me some of the animal meds from the cabinets that he assured me were fine for human consumption.

Finally, the good doctor had left, and then – not long after – Talia, Kane and I had too, not wishing to be on-site when the rest of the Badrock team returned from their all-expenses paid night out in Vegas.

We'd taken a jeep and driven west, burning out the branded vehicle in the desert and stealing an SUV from a long term parking lot in Flagstaff before continuing onto Las Vegas. It was the biggest city in the area and – with its constant stream of tourists – an easy place to get lost in.

Talia and I hired a motel room that took dogs, and used the time to try and recover. Kane did a faster job than me, back on his feet and raring to go within forty-eight hours, all but ignoring the large hole in his body.

Talia wanted to stay with me, but – despite my protective feelings for her – I advised her that it really wasn't a good idea. With my lifestyle, I wasn't a long-term relationship kind of guy. Hell, I wasn't a *short*-term relationship kind of guy, and we parted as friends after the third day, Talia promising me that she would try and rebuild her life.

I didn't know what she was going to do. Return home and claim her inheritance? Or disavow all connections with her father and move on completely?

Either way, her life would be easier now without him.

But I knew that my job wasn't completely over.

Not yet anyway.

"The name of the man who killed your boyfriend is Manfred Yates," I told Kayden over the phone.

It was part of the information that Talia had dug up on her father's computer – a list of clients, and the "prey" they had killed.

Yates had paid a million dollars to put a bullet in Benjamin "T.J." Hooker, and I thought that Kayden ought to know about it.

I wasn't sure what else to do with the information – as I've already said, getting it to the wrong people could end up with terminal results.

But I thought that this was a good start.

Kayden had paid me a thousand dollars for the truth, and this was it.

"What you choose to do with that information is up to you," I said, before putting the phone down and walking off down the hot sidewalk, Kane limping at my heel.

I was feeling the pain from my own wounds less now, and I was certainly in better shape than I'd been in after Iraq. I stopped in the street for a moment, the thought giving me pause. In that village near Mosul, I'd killed twenty-seven men and been called a hero, awarded the Medal of Honor by congress. They had been enemies of the United States, but they had been honest men at least, fighting for their homes, their families, a cause they believed in.

On that ranch in New Mexico I'd killed over thirty people, men and women both, and they had arguably deserved it far more than those poor saps in Iraq. They hadn't been fighting for a cause, they'd wanted to kill purely for killing's sake; and yet in this case there would be no medals for me, justifiable though my actions might have been. If caught, there would only be life in prison, plain and simple.

But that, I figured, was the life I'd chosen for myself.

There was no fighting it.

I wondered, as I carried on down the street, what sort of life Kayden would choose for herself.

Would she let it go?

Or would she pursue it, as I would?

I couldn't help but wonder what fate would befall Mr. Manfred Yates.

If it was anything like what happened to General Roman Badrock, then I could be sure of one thing.

Justice would have been well and truly served.

But not everyone, I reflected as we turned onto the Strip, was like me.

And I guess that's why I always have so much work.

THE END

. . . but Colt Ryder will return in
THE THOUSAND DOLLAR ESCAPE

ABOUT THE AUTHOR

J.T. Brannan is the author of the Amazon bestselling political thriller series featuring Mark Cole, as well as the high-concept thrillers ORIGIN (translated into eight languages in over thirty territories) and EXTINCTION (his latest all-action novel from Headline Publishing), in addition to the psychological crime thriller RED MOON RISING.

THE THOUSAND DOLLAR MAN – the first novel to feature his new hero, Colt Ryder – was nominated for the 2016 Killer Nashville Silver Falchion Award.

Currently serving in the British Army Reserves, J.T. Brannan is a former national Karate champion and bouncer.

He now writes full-time, and teaches martial arts in Harrogate, in the North of England, where he lives with his wife and two young children.

He is currently working on the next novel in the bestselling Mark Cole series, as well as further books in the all-new Colt Ryder series.

You can find him at www.jtbrannan.com and www.jtbrannanbooks.blogspot.com, on Twitter @JTBrannan_, and on Facebook at jtbrannanbooks.

ALSO BY THE AUTHOR

The Colt Ryder series:
THE THOUSAND DOLLAR MAN
THE THOUSAND DOLLAR HUNT
THE THOUSAND DOLLAR ESCAPE
THE THOUSAND DOLLAR CONTRACT

The Mark Cole series:
STOP AT NOTHING
WHATEVER THE COST
BEYOND ALL LIMITS
NEVER SAY DIE
PLEDGE OF HONOR
THE LONE PATRIOT

Alternative Mark Cole thriller:
SEVEN DAY HERO

Other Novels:
RED MOON RISING
ORIGIN
EXTINCTION
TIME QUEST

Short Story:
DESTRUCTIVE THOUGHTS

Made in United States
North Haven, CT
19 February 2022

16279950R00131